OFF GRID AND OFF LIMITS

JENNI FLETCHER

Recycling programs for this product may not exist in your area.

ISBN-13: 978-1-335-47082-9

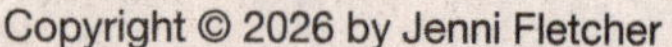

Off Grid and Off Limits

For questions and comments about the quality of this book, please contact us at CustomerService@Harlequin.com.

Harlequin Enterprises ULC
22 Adelaide St. West, 41st Floor
Toronto, Ontario M5H 4E3, Canada
www.Harlequin.com

HarperCollins Publishers
Macken House, 39/40 Mayor Street Upper,
Dublin 1, D01 C9W8, Ireland
www.HarperCollins.com

Printed in U.S.A.

1 2 3 4 5 6 7 8 9 10 HDC 28 27 26 25

"Why don't you come to the race this weekend and see what you think?" Dario suggested. "I'll go as fast as I can. Just for you."

He chuckled and held a hand out. "What do you say, Ms. Thorne? Do we have a deal?"

"Livi." She seemed to take a deep breath before wrapping her fingers around his. "And yes, we have a deal."

"Good." He stiffened, surprised by a sudden buzz of heat, like electricity shooting up his arm. If he wasn't mistaken, her pupils flared at the same moment, as if she felt it too, before she yanked her hand away again.

"That's settled then." She spun on her heel, practically running away from him toward the door. "I'll go and find Camille."

"Good idea." He flexed his fingers. He had no idea what had just happened, but now it seemed he had two objectives for the weekend—to win the race and to convince her.

He wasn't sure which was going to be the bigger challenge.

Jenni Fletcher was born in the north of Scotland and now lives in Yorkshire with her husband and two children. She wanted to be a writer as a child but became distracted by reading instead, finally getting past her first paragraph thirty years later. She's had more jobs than she can remember but has finally found one she loves. She can be contacted on Instagram @jennifletcherauthor or via her Facebook author page.

Books by Jenni Fletcher

Off Grid and Off Limits
is Jenni Fletcher's debut title for Love Always.

Harlequin Historical

Highland Alliances

The Highlander's Tactical Marriage

Regency Belles of Bath

An Unconventional Countess
Unexpectedly Wed to the Officer
The Duke's Runaway Bride
The Shopgirl's Forbidden Love

Secrets of a Victorian Household

Miss Amelia's Mistletoe Marquess

Sons of Sigurd

Redeeming Her Viking Warrior

The Christmas Runaway
A Marriage Made in Secret
A Wedding to Protect Her Fortune
A Marquess to Remember

Visit the Author Profile page
at Harlequin.com for more titles.

For Andy, my favorite driver

CHAPTER ONE

'DARIO XYDIS? Is this a joke?' Livi Thorne stared across her agent's solid oak desk in dismay. She'd come into the office to discuss a biography of Erin Cole, Irish pop legend, not some playboy racing driver.

'No joke.' Camille stared back, unperturbed. 'His team are offering good money, and I mean *really* good.'

'I don't care! You got me here under false pretences.'

'Only because I knew you'd refuse to discuss it otherwise.'

'That's no excuse.' Livi folded her arms across her chest indignantly. 'You know that writing Erin's biography is basically my dream project.'

'I do, which is why I wasn't lying entirely. From what I've heard, she really *is* looking for a biographer, but not until her world tour finishes at the end of the year. A book on Dario Xydis would keep you busy in the meantime.'

'No, thank you. I'd rather write a biography of…' Livi glanced over her shoulder for inspiration, through the glass wall at the open-plan office beyond. 'Literally, anyone in there!'

'Fascinating as the lives of my staff undoubtedly are, the reading public might not be quite so interested.' Camille sat forward, pressing her perfectly manicured fingertips together while adopting her most be-reasonable expression. 'Look, I know Xydis isn't the kind of person you normally write about, but just take a moment to think about it.'

'I don't want—'

'*One* moment.'

'Fine.' Livi placed a hand on her sternum, drawing in a deep breath before letting it out again in an exasperated rush. 'No. No way. When have I ever shown any interest in cars, let alone motor racing?'

'The book would be about his life, not engines and regulations. I mean, obviously you'd have to learn a little about motorsport, but that's a small price to pay for a guaranteed bestseller, which is what this is. Everyone thinks he's going to win the World Championship this year, and with a British team, too. That means an official biography will be in every bookstore in the country, and it could have *your* name on the cover. Honestly, opportunities like this don't come along very often. Most writers would be biting my hand off.'

'Then I guess I'm not most writers.' Livi tossed her newly blonde hair emphatically. 'Camille, you know how I work. I need to feel inspired and excited about my subjects. There has to be *some* kind of emotional investment, and I'm sorry, but I just can't bring myself to care about some racing driver. You'll have to find somebody else to write it.'

'I would.' Camille tugged at the cuffs of her boucle Chanel jacket, the exact same shade as her caramel tortoiseshell highlights. 'Only according to his manager, he doesn't want anybody else. He wants you.'

'Me?' Livi blinked, shocked to discover that Dario Xydis was even aware of her existence. 'Why?'

'Presumably he's read some of your work and thinks you're impartial and empathetic.'

'I *am* impartial and empathetic.' She gritted her teeth at the implication. 'Just not towards men who cheat on their wives. I don't know much about him, but I know that. You couldn't even glance online a couple of years ago without reading some story about all his affairs, and I refuse to work with a cheater.'

'O-kay.' Camille sat back in her black leather chair, the one that made her look like a Bond villain minus the fluffy white cat, a knowing expression on her face. 'Do you think maybe there's a chance you're transferring some of your feelings about Matthew onto him?'

'Maybe.' Livi stiffened as a familiar ache gripped her chest. 'Although I don't think that's so unreasonable.'

'It's not. I get it, your fiancé left you for that other woman, what was her name again?'

'Sienna.'

'Right, Sienna. That must have been a horrible shock, but what was it, two months ago now? Plus, you're obviously doing okay. You look amazing.'

Livi forced a smile. Her life had actually imploded just one month ago, and the only reason she looked amazing was that she hadn't wanted Camille to think she was too much of a mess to work with Erin. Ironically, *that* was the reason she'd booked herself an emergency salon session the day before, treating herself to a HydraFacial and French manicure before impulsively cutting and dyeing her long, light brown hair a shoulder-length sunflower blonde. She was even wearing her best black Reiss suit with a collarless petal pink blouse underneath. Now she couldn't help wishing she'd come with dull skin, split ends and in her pyjamas instead.

'Thanks.' She unclenched her jaw with an effort. 'But I just can't deal with any kind of toxic masculinity right now.'

'Toxic is a little harsh.' Camille's tone was faintly chiding. 'There haven't been any more scandals since Xydis's divorce. Admittedly, he's developed something of a reputation for difficult behaviour, but that's all.'

'Fine, I retract the word "toxic".' Livi sighed before tilting her head. 'And what do you mean by "difficult behaviour"?'

'It's hard to explain.' Camille's brow furrowed. 'I mean, he was never exactly afraid of expressing his opinions. The press actually used to love him for it, but now he's abrasive too, always arguing and taking offence in interviews, like he's determined to make enemies of them. Whoever's in charge of his media training must tear their hair out on a weekly basis, but on the plus side, a huge number of fans still support him and he's always incredibly generous with them.'

'So he's an egotist as well as a cheater?'

'I didn't say *that*.' Camille lifted her eyes to the ceiling. 'Look, as your friend, I feel bad about pushing this, but as your agent, I'm trying to do what's best for your career and, trust me, this is it. You've made a decent name for yourself with your past few books, but this will send your profile through the roof, which is exactly what you need if you want Erin Cole to choose you as her biographer. If you do a good job with this, her people might actually come to *us*.' She leaned forward across the desk. 'Come on, it's not like you're working on anything else right now. You wrapped up your last project a few weeks ago.'

'Because I was supposed to be getting married this weekend!' Livi squeezed her fists together so tightly, she could feel her fingernails digging into her palms. 'You know how hard I worked to clear my schedule in time for the wedding. I was going to look for a new project after the honeymoon.'

'Well, now you don't have to look. You can get started straight away, which you'll need to because the schedule for this is intense. Xydis's management want the book published to coincide with the end of the racing season in December, which means a first draft by late September. They already have a publisher, but they want to choose their own writer.'

Livi's jaw dropped open. 'They want me to write a biography in under three months?'

'With a final draft the month after. Obviously, nobody expected him to do so well this year so the whole thing's a bit of a rush job, but they must be hoping he'll have the World Championship in the bag by then.' Camille's unruffled expression didn't falter. 'The idea is for you to make a start with the research now, then head to Monaco with Xydis for the summer break at the start of August. He has an apartment there apparently. More importantly, according to the rules, he's prohibited from doing anything driving-related during that time, so you'll have total access for a whole ten days. It's completely insane, but if anyone can do it, it's you. You're one of the best biographers I know and you're fast. Plus, I know you love a challenge.' She glanced sideways at the sound of a knock. 'Yes?'

'Sorry to interrupt, Camille.' A man with spiky auburn hair stuck his head through the door. 'You told me to let you know when it was time for Naomi's birthday cake.'

'I'll just be a minute.' She gave him a quick nod before pushing her chair back and looking meaningfully at Livi. 'Time to go and be a good boss. Don't go anywhere, okay?'

'Only if you promise to bring me some cake.'

'Well, obviously.'

Livi smiled weakly, waiting until her agent had gone before throwing her head back, opening her mouth wide in a silent scream, and then reaching into her vintage black leather satchel for her phone.

A quick search and skim-read later, and she had to concede that Dario Andreas Xydis was at least somewhat more interesting than she'd initially given him credit for. Although he'd been born in Thessaloniki in Greece, his family had emigrated to Sydney, Australia when he was still a baby, giving him dual citizenship and guaranteeing a degree of fan loyalty in both hemispheres. Career-wise, he'd started karting aged six, won a national championship at thirteen, then moved into single seat racing when he was fifteen. Now, seventeen years later, he was a member of the racing elite, one of the best of the best, although until recently he'd never had a car capable of delivering the World Championship. The closest he'd come was two years before, when he'd dominated the first half of the season, only to suffer a dramatic drop in performance when the rumours about his *many* extra-marital affairs had become public.

This year, however, he seemed to be in a different league to the rest of the grid. Even his teammate couldn't get within two seconds of his finish times. With eight races under his belt, and another sixteen to go, all the pundits were saying it was his championship to lose. Obviously, he was riding high and wanted a biography to capitalise on it.

Well, she couldn't blame him for that, but why the hell did he want *her* to write it? Her previous books had done reasonably well, but she wasn't exactly in the big leagues, not yet anyway. She probably ought to feel flattered, but frankly, being headhunted for this project was more of an inconvenience. She wrote about people she admired and was enthusiastic about, which generally meant strong, empowered women, not overpaid, overhyped drivers whose only interests in life appeared to be fast cars and lingerie models. As far as she could tell, Dario Xydis was basically a walking cliché, with numerous sponsorship deals, homes in Monaco, Sydney and Athens, and the kind of striking good looks normally reserved for Hollywood actors.

Despite herself, she found her gaze lingering on his photos, taking in the striking combination of sharp jaw, lustrous dark hair, thick black brows and huge, liquid brown eyes. Everything about him screamed heart-throb, though no doubt he was aware of the fact. He was probably the type of man who thought he could get any woman he wanted, to do anything he wanted.

Like write his official biography.

Urgh! She tossed her phone back into her

satchel with a snort of contempt. Puppy dog eyes aside, he was exactly the kind of man she hated. 'Difficult', unfaithful and, given his choice of career, obviously suffering from an over-abundance of testosterone. There was no way she wanted to spend so much as a minute in his company, but Camille was right, objectively speaking, this *was* a great opportunity. The money would definitely be useful—she couldn't avoid thinking about her dwindling bank balance much longer—and maybe anything would be better than moping about in her flat, eating her way through four boxes' worth of heart-shaped and non-returnable white chocolate and honeycomb wedding favours. It would make a lot more sense to throw herself back into work, to bury her feelings until hopefully she didn't feel them any longer. Then at least her career would still be a success even if the rest of her life was in turmoil. And if it helped to get Erin Cole's attention…

Could she really say no to that?

She tapped her thumb against her bottom lip, knowing what her ten-year-old self, dancing around her bedroom to Erin's music, would tell her to do. Erin had been her favourite artist then, and for the almost two decades since, a singer, songwriter and role model with a huge voice, a poetic soul and a seemingly inexhaustible ability to reinvent herself no matter what the world or media threw at her, so the idea of writing her biography, of spending time with her… It would be a dream come true, the absolute pinnacle of Livi's career so far, not to mention a way of recalibrating her own life. If anyone could teach her how to pick herself up and start again after Matthew's betrayal, it was Erin, whose own troubled love life was practically legendary. In other words, she *needed* to get that contract. And all she had to do was devote the rest of the year to Dario Xydis, infamous love rat…

A shudder ran through her at the thought. She didn't know if she could bear the irony, let alone be fair and impartial.

'So?' Camille walked back into the office a few moments later. 'What do you say?'

'Where's my cake?'

'In the kitchen. I'm withholding until you agree to meet Dario.'

'Wow. Manipulative much?'

'I didn't get where I am by being nice.'

'You could have told me that before I signed with you.' Livi pinched the bridge of her nose with a groan. 'Isn't there *any* other high-profile project I could work on?'

'Not right now.'

'Will you drop me as a client if I refuse?'

'No.' Camille perched on the edge of her desk. 'I'll just be disappointed that you judged the man without even meeting him. I thought you were more open-minded than that.'

'That's a low blow.'

'Again, this is my job.'

'Do you really think it would help me get the Erin Cole contract?'

'I honestly do.'

'Fine.' She sagged back in her chair, defeated. 'I'll meet him, but I'm not making any promises.'

'That's all I ask.'

'But I'm not happy about it.'

'Noted.' Camille pushed herself back off the desk. 'Come on. He's waiting in the conference room.'

'What?' Livi dropped a hand to her stomach as it lurched violently. 'He's here? Now?'

'Yes, he arrived five minutes ago. This project has a tight turnaround, I told you.' Camille was already halfway back to the door. 'That means, the sooner the two of you meet, the better. Then, if all goes well, we can get down to the nitty gritty of the contract.'

'Wait! Did you just set me up?' Livi gasped. '*Is* there any birthday cake or was that some kind of code?'

'Oh, there's cake, but we sang *Happy Birth-*

day to Naomi this morning.' Camille's smile was borderline smug. 'Let's just say, I'd knew you'd see sense. Now, let's go. You don't want to keep a future world champion waiting.'

CHAPTER TWO

HE SHOULD NEVER have agreed to this.

Dario glowered at the conference room door, wondering what would happen if he simply got up and walked out. Probably not much to begin with. Ethan might not even notice at first. A surreptitious glance showed his manager still marching back and forth beside the floor-to-ceiling windows, ignoring the dynamic London skyline in favour of his phone's constantly flashing screen. Optimistically, he probably had about five minutes to escape, after which he could do any one of the hundred other, more useful things he *ought* to be doing right now, like getting in some more simulator time at his team HQ or discussing strategy with his race engineer—things that would actually help his World Championship chances, unlike this, sitting in a literary agency waiting to discuss a biography of all things, as if the rest of the world had any right to his personal life.

Screw it. He rubbed a hand over his unshaven jaw, already pushing his chair back. People could say what they liked about him—they usually did anyway—but his focus needed to be on the present, not the past, especially when this whole project had the potential to cause more harm than good. His driving could speak for itself, and if people didn't appreciate that, they could—

'Don't even think about it.'

'What?' He froze halfway out of his chair.

'You know what.' Ethan's gaze was still fixed on his phone. 'Don't think I'm not prepared to wrestle you to the floor and sit on you if it keeps you here.'

'Please.' He gave a disparaging snort. 'I've seen you in the gym. You wouldn't stand a chance.'

'Don't push me.' Ethan's gaze finally flicked upwards. 'Dario, you're at the peak of your career. That means people are paying attention to you right now. After all the malicious comments and negativity of the past two years, you have a chance to shift the public's attention away from your personal life and back to your career as an elite athlete. This is a golden opportunity to rehabilitate your image and define your own legacy. Don't throw it away.' He dropped into the chair beside him. 'More importantly, if you don't write this book, somebody else will, and unless you want to be remembered as a pig-headed, argumentative philanderer, I highly suggest that you sit back down.'

'Great pep talk.' Dario subsided back into his chair. 'Thanks.'

'Just saving you from yourself.' Ethan tapped his phone one last time before tucking it away. 'Come on, you're the one who wanted to meet this…what was her name again?'

'Livi Thorne.'

'Right, Livi Thorne, when I had about a dozen sports journalists all queuing up to work on this project, any one of whom would have been a better choice, by the way.'

'You managed to find a sports journalist I *haven't* argued with?' Dario shot him a sceptical look.

'No, but a few of them were prepared to overlook the fact. What's so great about this writer anyway? As far as I can tell, she has no connection to any sport, let alone driving. Are you a fan of her books or something?'

'No. I'm more into thrillers.'

'So why are we here again?'

'Because she was recommended to me by somebody who *has* read her books.' Dario leaned back, unfastening the buttons on his black herringbone jacket. 'They say she's talented and I trust their judgement.'

'*And?*'

'And that's pretty much all I know about her, but if I have to do this then I want someone good.'

'Seriously? That's it?'

'Gentlemen. Sorry to keep you waiting, but we're ready now.' Camille Colston, the literary agent who'd met them in the lobby five minutes earlier, marched through the door at that moment, accompanied by another, shorter woman with summery blonde hair, a diamond-shaped face and the largest, most vividly green eyes he'd ever seen. Everything about her looked poised and professional, from her neat, sleek chignon to her perfectly fitting trouser suit, to her finely sculpted brows, currently drawn together in a frown.

Wait… He sat up a little straighter. *This* was Livi Thorne?

First impression: not what he'd expected. Second impression: cute. Third impression: she didn't want to be there.

Well, this was ironic. Apparently, they had something in common.

'Ms Thorne.' He stood up, flashing a wide smile as he extended a hand across the table.

'I'm Dario Xydis. It's a pleasure to meet you. This is my manager, Ethan Duchamp.'

'Mr Xydis, Mr Duchamp.' She gave a tight smile in reply, placing her fingers in his for the shortest amount of time possible before yanking them away again, her posture rigid.

'Shall we all take a seat?' Camille's tone was arguably a little too perky. 'Are you sure you wouldn't like coffee?'

'We're fine.' Ethan waved a hand, getting straight down to business as they sat on opposite sides of a sixteen-seater conference table. 'Before we discuss terms, I think it's best that we address the proposed timescale. Ms Thorne, I've put together a document containing basic autobiographical information, including the key dates and details of Dario's career, but there's obviously still a significant amount of research to be done. Do you think you're capable of handling all that and producing a manuscript to such a tight deadline?'

'It's not ideal, but yes.' She pulled her shoulders back, as if she were offended by the question. 'However, just to be clear, this is only a preliminary discussion regarding the *possibility* of me writing this biography. Personally, I'm not convinced that Mr Xydis and I would be the best fit.'

'Really?' Dario draped an arm across the empty seat beside him. 'Why's that?'

Green eyes flickered in his direction. 'For one thing, I've never written about a sports personality before. It's not exactly my area of expertise. For another, we might have different ideas about which parts of your life are significant.' She paused, tapping a French tip nail on the table before continuing. 'Or maybe I simply won't find your story interesting enough to pursue.'

He gave an abrupt laugh. 'Lots of people seem to think motor sports are pretty interesting. More than five hundred million, globally.'

'Racing might be, but this book would be about *you*.' She held his gaze. 'I'm interested in psychology, not engines.'

He quirked an eyebrow, trying to make sense of the waves of passive aggression radiating across the table. Her voice sounded perfectly calm and composed and yet the undertone of tension in the room was palpable, like the buzz of electricity before a storm. Okay, so apparently it wasn't the sports element of the book she objected to. It was him. Interesting. He knew his reputation had taken a pretty severe hit with all the rumours surrounding his divorce two years ago, but surely that wasn't enough to justify this level of hostility, especially in a business meeting. Whatever her issue was, it felt personal somehow.

Suddenly he didn't want to leave the room any longer. She was far too intriguing for that. Not to mention hot, in an uptight, highly-strung, sexy librarian kind of way. He felt a powerful urge to loosen her up a bit.

'In other words, you're suggesting I don't have enough depth for a biography?' He sat forward in his chair.

'I'm sure that's not what Livi meant,' Camille intervened.

'I've no idea if you have depth or not.' Ms Thorne ignored her. 'But you should know that I value the truth, the *whole* truth, not some air-brushed, sanitised version where you get to play the hero. I'm not interested in personal branding or vanity projects. If I *were* to write your biography, I'd need you to be completely honest and transparent with me.'

'Wait a moment.' Ethan held a hand up, palm outwards. 'We're not paying for some hatchet job.'

'Hatchet job?' She opened her eyes wide, until they looked almost impossibly huge. 'Is the truth really that bad?'

'No, but there would need to be some boundaries. Obviously, my client will be honest, but within reason.'

'Boundary. Just one,' Dario corrected him. 'My marriage, including my divorce. That's not something I'm prepared to discuss.'

'Surely you're not suggesting I leave it out completely?' There was an incredulous edge to her voice now. 'That's impossible. It was a huge story.'

'I remember, but I don't want it brought up again. Other than that, I'll tell you anything about my life you want to know.'

'And that's non-negotiable?'

'Completely.'

'What a shame.' Long black lashes dipped, sweeping out over her cheeks, though not quickly enough to hide the flash of triumph in her gaze. 'In that case, I'm afraid this discussion is over.'

'Fine with us.' Ethan made to stand up. 'We can find another writer by the end of the day.'

'You know, I think I would like that coffee,' Dario interrupted, smiling across the table at Camille. 'Would you mind?'

'Oh…' The agent's eyebrows shot up. 'Of course. I'll just be a minute.'

'Take your time.' He turned towards Ethan. 'This might actually be a good opportunity for the two of you to discuss the advance. I don't think we were being generous enough. Say another ten percent?'

'*Ten?*'

'Hold on.' Ms Thorne was frowning at him again. 'Mr Xydis, this isn't about the money.'

'Call me Dario, and you're right. Twenty percent.' He rested an elbow on his chair arm, ignoring Ethan's furious look as Camille closed the door behind them. 'That's better. Now we can talk properly.'

'Why?' She sounded as if she were speaking through gritted teeth. 'I've already given you my answer.'

'Yet you're still here.'

'Only because if I walk out, my agent might be angry enough to drop me.' Her nostrils flared. 'Did you really have to add another twenty percent?'

'Sorry.' He gave her a distinctly unapologetic grin. 'But you know, if you really wanted out of this project, you went about it completely the wrong way. You should have flattered me, told me what a big fan you are. Playing hard to get only brings out my competitive side. It makes me want to change your mind.'

Her expression shuttered. 'I don't play games.'

'I can see that. So, tell me, what exactly have I done to offend you?'

'Nothing.'

He gave her a critical look. 'I thought you

said you valued the truth? It seems like I've definitely done something.'

'Mr Xydis—'

'Dario.'

'Dario. You've been nothing but polite and courteous since we met. What possible reason could I have to be offended?'

'Good point…' He rubbed his knuckles across his chin. 'All right, I'll rephrase. Why don't you like me?'

She gave an incredulous laugh. 'I don't know you!'

'But you don't like me. It was obvious the moment you entered the room. I'm simply curious about the reason.'

She hesitated, catching her bottom lip between her teeth, as if she was trying to decide whether or not to answer. For a moment, he thought she was on the verge of telling him, before she lowered her gaze and shook her head. 'Mr Xydis—Dario—I think you're mistaking our roles. *I'm* the potential biographer, *you're* the subject. That means I'm the one who gets to ask questions.'

'Ah.' He let his gaze roam over her face, over her high cheekbones and slightly pointed chin. 'That's a shame. You seem like you might give some interesting answers.'

A rush of heat swept up her neck and across

those same cheekbones as she surged to her feet, walking across to the windows as if the effort of biting her lip was suddenly too great. 'You know, if you really think I don't like you, it makes absolutely no sense for me to write your biography. I might be biased.'

'Nice try, but I don't think so.' He leaned further back in his chair. 'You're too good at what you do. "Smart, perceptive and balanced", that's what I was told.'

'Who by?' She looked back over her shoulder, as if she were reluctantly interested.

'Somebody I trust. Which means, whether you like me or not, you'll do a fair job.'

She made a soft sound, something between a sigh and a snort, before turning away again. 'You must really trust their opinion.'

'I do.' He got up too, casually sliding his hands into his suit pockets as he went to stand beside her. 'Okay, you say you value honesty. Would it help to know I'm not exactly thrilled by this "vanity project" either?'

'It might.' She gave him a suspicious look. 'Why aren't you?'

'Because I have a World Championship to win. That's where my focus ought to be, and I don't particularly relish the idea of sharing my private life with the world either. Unfortunately, my reputation isn't as good as it used to be. I've antagonised too many people, the press especially. It's given me a reputation for being a little…'

'Difficult?' Her eyes flashed again.

'That's one way to put it. The upshot is that now the media likes to paint me as the villain of the sport, which doesn't exactly impress my sponsors.' He grimaced. 'Ethan thinks I need to take back the narrative and define my legacy before somebody else does.'

'In other words, you want me to rehabilitate your image?' An expression of distaste crossed her features.

'I'd like to give my side of the story, that's all.' He felt a flicker of irritation. 'I think I'm entitled to that much, especially since this might be my last chance at the championship.'

'Why?'

He lifted his shoulders. 'I'm thirty-two. There's no guarantee I'll still have a seat next year even if I do win the championship.'

'Thirty-two isn't exactly old. Some drivers carry on into their forties, don't they?'

'Yes, but there are still hundreds of talented kids out there, every one of them itching to take my seat. One of these years, one of them will get it.'

'Fair enough…' Her expression softened slightly. 'But how exactly do you expect me to give your side of the story when there's a big part of it you won't talk about? From what I've read, your relationship with the press deteriorated *after* the collapse of your marriage.' She gave him a pointed look. 'Some people might say that's your villain origin story.'

'I was married for one year out of a seventeen-year professional racing career. Isn't the rest enough for a biography?' He rolled his eyes at her intractable expression. 'Fine. If it matters that much, you can use any information already in the public record, but I absolutely won't discuss it, and I don't want anyone invading my ex-wife's privacy by approaching her either.'

'In other words, whatever's in the public record is true?' Her eyes narrowed.

'I didn't say that.'

'But surely you want to correct any misinformation?'

He gritted his teeth, aware of a muscle twitching in his jaw. It was an unfortunate habit whenever the subject of his divorce came up. 'I simply want certain aspects of my past to stay in the past.'

'I think you're forgetting what a biography is.'

'A *sporting* biography. All I ask is that you focus on my driving.'

'Then maybe you should ask somebody who

knows about cars!' She sounded exasperated. 'Would I be allowed total creative control?'

'Sure, if you think Ethan would ever agree to that. How about, both sides have to agree on a draft?'

Her brows puckered. 'That sounds...feasible.'

'Good.' He nodded slowly, surprised by how determined he was to convince her. Considering her antipathy and their shared lack of enthusiasm for the project, it made about as much sense to him as it obviously did to her. He just had the strangest feeling that, now they'd met, no other writer would do.

'I tell you what...' He tore his gaze away from her face, realising he'd been staring a little too long. 'Why don't you come to the race this weekend and see what you think? You can meet some people, do a little research, ask a few questions. No strings, no commitment, all expenses paid, VIP hospitality. Then, if you're still not interested, I'll tell your agent it's my decision, not yours.'

'*This* weekend?' There was a strange crack in her voice, accompanied by an almost pained expression, as if he'd just said something deliberately hurtful. For a couple of seconds, she looked so wounded, he felt an instinctive, albeit quickly suppressed, urge to reach out and wrap her in his arms.

'Yes.' He paused. 'Unless...do you already have plans?'

'No.' She gave a visible swallow, the word seeming to hitch in her throat. 'I did, but...they changed. Where's the race?'

'Barcelona. Spain. I'll get my assistant to arrange everything, so all you have to do is watch.' He smiled softly. 'If you think you can bear it?'

'That depends.' She didn't smile back. 'How long do races usually take?'

'About two hours.'

'*Two hours?*' She looked as horrified as if he'd just told her that she had to drive in it too.

'I'll go as fast as I can. Just for you.' He chuckled and held a hand out. 'What do you say, Ms Thorne? Do we have a deal?'

'It's Livi.' She looked down at his hand, taking a deep breath before wrapping her fingers around it. 'And yes, we have a deal.'

'Good.' He stiffened, surprised by a sudden buzz of heat, like a pulse of electricity shooting up his arm. If he wasn't mistaken, her pupils flared at the same moment, as if she felt it too, before she yanked her hand and her gaze away again.

'That's settled then.' She spun on her heel, practically running away from him towards the door. 'I'll go and find Camillc.'

'Good idea.' He looked down at his hand and

flexed his fingers. He had no idea what had just happened, but now it seemed he had two objectives for the weekend—to win the race and to convince her.

He wasn't sure which was going to be the bigger challenge.

CHAPTER THREE

'OW!' LIVI SQUEAKED as expert fingers kneaded their way up her spine and into her shoulder blades. 'That hurts!'

'I'm not surprised.' Her sister Chloe pushed her back down as she tried to wriggle off the massage table. 'Seriously, what have you done to yourself? Your neck is like a solid block of tension.'

'Hmm, I wonder why? If only there was some kind of recent, emotionally devastating event to explain it.' She winced at her own sarcasm. 'Sorry. Painful as this is, thanks for fitting me in. I really needed it after my meeting today.'

'It's okay. I had a cancellation, but you know, if this is how you treat your body, you should seriously consider booking a regular treatment.'

'I will, I promise.' She sucked in a deep breath, letting it out again slowly as tension oozed from her muscles. Having a physiotherapist for a little sister was definitely useful, even if most people needed to see a birth certificate to believe they were actually related. Where she was short and fair, Chloe was tall and dark; where she was happy to sit at a desk all day, Chloe couldn't bear to be still for more than two minutes at a time. Just about the only things they had in common were green eyes and a shared love of Erin Cole.

'So let me see if I've got this straight,' Chloe went on, scrunching her fingers into Livi's rigid neck muscles. 'Your agent says that if you write the Xydis book, you'll have a better chance of being hired by Erin?'

'Pretty much.'

'Then you have to do it! Remember how obsessed you were with her *Sailing Away* album when you were fourteen? You played it for about three months straight. Dad said he forgot what you looked like without headphones.'

'I was going through stuff! My first boyfriend had just dumped me. And you were obsessed, too,' Livi protested, conveniently omitting the fact that she'd listened to that same album on her way over.

'Not *that* much.'

'I guess not.' She sighed. 'The thing is, I'd love to meet her, even if it's just so I can tell her how much her music means to me, but I wish there was some other way. It's not like I can just dial in the Xydis book. I'd have to do it properly, which would mean a lot of time and energy on a subject I'm not remotely excited about.' She grimaced at a particularly loud crunching sound. 'I've never written a book I didn't care about before, and the weirdest thing is, I practically told him I wasn't interested and it didn't even bother him. He just seemed to think I'd do a decent job anyway.'

'Because you would. And even if you're not excited about it, just imagine how Matthew will feel when he finds out you're spending the summer with a hot racing driver.'

'There's no way for him to find out. It's not like we're communicating much any more. We even unfollowed each other's social media because it seemed like the healthy thing to do.'

'He'd hear about it somehow, trust me. Stuff like this always gets out.'

'I still doubt he'd care, not now he has Sienna.'

'Then maybe you should find somebody new as well?'

'No, thank you.' She felt her shoulders tense all over again. 'From now on, I'm swearing off men and focusing on my career. My work is just about the only thing in my life Matthew didn't wreck.'

'You can't give up on relationships completely. What about Xydis?' Chloe's fingers squeezed tighter. 'He's gorgeous.'

'He's also a cheating scumbag!' She hurled the words a little more forcefully than she'd intended, but the truth was, meeting Dario in person had left her feeling a little…confused. As much as she detested him as a cheater, he'd also been the most devastatingly attractive man she'd ever set eyes on, obviously in peak physical condition, with a raw masculinity and charisma that his photos hadn't adequately prepared her for. He'd even smelled amazing, musky with a citrusy undertone and just the faintest hint of smoky vanilla. And as for his eyes… Up close, they'd actually been two different colours, both shades of brown, but where one was dark chocolate, the other had contained flecks of rich amber. There had been something magnetic about them, especially coupled with his deep, velvety Australian accent when he'd told her she was smart and fair and been so insistent on her writing the book, as if she were somehow special.

His insistence had been particularly confusing considering how badly she'd behaved. She'd hardly recognised herself during their conversation, inwardly cringing at her own rude, confrontational behaviour while being completely unable to do anything about it. Her terrible attitude would have got her thrown out of most meetings, and yet he'd almost seemed to enjoy it.

Worst of all had been the moment when he'd invited her to the race that weekend, on the day that ought to have been her wedding day, and she'd almost burst into tears—as if she hadn't already cried herself out over the past month! She'd suppressed the impulse, barely, but the intense way he'd looked at her had seemed to penetrate straight through her defences, right into her heart and soul, in a way that nobody ever had before, not even Matthew.

As for the sudden jolt of electricity she'd felt when she'd taken his hand, a searing heat that had radiated outwards until every part of her body had been flushed and tingling...well, she absolutely refused to think about *that*.

'Anyway...' She coughed, adjusting her tone before Chloe could accuse her of protesting too much. 'Even if he wasn't a cheating scumbag, I could never get involved with somebody I was writing about. It would completely undermine my professional integrity.'

'Urgh, you're so good.' She could practically hear Chloe rolling her eyes.

'*And* I'm not exactly racing driver girlfriend material. This isn't some fairy tale. A man like Dario Xydis could have his pick of beautiful women.'

'Hey.' Chloe's hands stilled. 'Don't do that. Don't put yourself down. You can't let Matthew undermine your confidence in yourself. You're beautiful too, and I love your new hair.'

Livi made a face. Subjectively, she knew that Chloe was right—not about the beautiful part, although she thought she was reasonably attractive—only believing it deep-down wasn't so easy, not any more. Matthew hadn't just undermined her confidence; he'd blown it to smithereens. And it was going to take a lot more than a new hair colour to fix that...

'Thanks, but it doesn't matter anyway. Like I said, he's a cheating scumbag.'

'*Is* he though?' Chloe sounded thoughtful. 'I remember there being some stuff about him in the tabloids a couple of years ago, but he never confirmed or denied anything, did he?'

'I've no idea, but he ended up divorced soon afterwards so there must have been some truth to the rumours.'

'Um, what about there being two sides to every story?'

'In his case, I don't care. I'm not in a mood to listen to excuses about how his wife misunderstood or neglected him.' She tightened her hands into fists at her sides and then released them again. 'I know how self-righteous and horrible I sound, and I know people sometimes have reasons for cheating, but it's not exactly my favourite subject right now. Although, to be fair, he's refusing to discuss his marriage anyway.'

'Well, that's perfect, isn't it? Then you won't have to discuss the subject of cheating.'

'You sound like Camille. I'd still have to spend ten whole days with him!'

'Right. In Monaco. Nightmare.'

Livi glared accusingly at her sister's bare feet under the table. Given the recent collapse of all her hopes and dreams for the future, was it *so* hard to understand that she didn't want to spend her summer with an infamous love cheat? It would be like a daily reminder of Matthew, the former love-of-her-life whose betrayal had completely blindsided her. They'd been together for seven years, ever since a mutual friend had set them up on a blind date, and lived together for the past six. She'd thought they were so compatible, sharing the same interests and values, enjoying the same foods, laughing at the same jokes. She'd thought they were happy. She'd thought that she'd known him. She definitely *hadn't* thought him capable of cheating.

He'd broken the news about Sienna one evening after dinner when they'd been settling down with a glass of red wine on the sofa, although she'd initially assumed it was some kind of bad joke. She'd known he'd been a little distracted for a few weeks beforehand, but she'd been so busy with her last book, she'd put it down to pre-wedding nerves. The idea of an affair had never once entered her head.

He hadn't understood what real love was until he met Sienna, he'd told her. Their attraction had been irresistible, like a force of nature, rendering him powerless to do anything but follow his heart. Of course, he still loved *her* too, but this new relationship was different, more intense, more physical.

She'd got up at that point and run to the bathroom, vomiting up the dinner they'd just eaten, feeling as though she'd just been pushed off a cliff by the person she'd trusted most in the world. Even now, there were times when she felt as though she was still falling.

Afterwards, she'd consoled herself that maybe it was true, that maybe Matthew and Sienna were soulmates and there had been nothing she could have done to save their own relationship. It was certainly better than accepting the alternative, that in the end, Sienna was just prettier and sexier—*better*—than her.

As if all that hadn't been enough, Matthew had blamed her too. Not directly, of course, but when he'd moved out, he'd *suggested* that her career had come between them, that she'd been so wrapped up in her work, she'd neglected their relationship. It had been all she could do not to push him out of their flat and slam the door in his face. It wasn't her *career* that had betrayed and devastated her! And if he thought she'd been absorbed before, she was going to be downright engrossed from now on. At least her *career* could be relied upon.

'Not to sound brutal…' Chloe's voice broke into her thoughts. 'But can you really afford to turn down this Xydis project? Didn't you say you'd lost a ton of money on the wedding?'

A lump of emotion mixed with panic rose in her throat at the reminder. She couldn't deny the money Xydis was offering was a pretty good incentive. The first thing she'd done after leaving Camille's office was look at her bank balance, which had led to some mild hyperventilating, followed by a few, quickly dashed away tears. If only Matthew had called their wedding off sooner, things wouldn't have been quite so bad. All of the deposits would still have been lost, but at least some of the balances wouldn't have been paid. As it was, they'd spent a small fortune on things that would never be used. And now Matthew had moved out of their flat there was no way she was going to be able to manage the rent on her own for much longer. She'd have to find somewhere new…unless she accepted Dario's offer, that was. It seemed a cruel irony that the only way to save herself from the financial mess left by her cheater of an ex-fiancé was to work with another cheater!

'I told you, you should have kept the ring.' Chloe clucked her tongue as she draped a towel over Livi's back and shoulders. 'There you go, all done.'

'Thanks.' She sat up and rolled her head in a circle. 'That feels so much better.'

'Good, because my fingers are strained from working out all those knots.' Chloe handed her a glass of water. 'Now drink this. Flush out the toxins or you'll get a migraine.'

'*Get* one?' Livi pressed a hand to her forehead. 'I feel like I've had a permanent headache for the past month.'

'Still not sleeping well?'

'Not even close. I've forgotten what it's like not to wake up ten times a night.'

'Oh, Liv.' Chloe wrapped her arms around her, enveloping her in a bear-hug. 'Look, can I give you my honest opinion?'

'Isn't that what you've been doing?'

'I'm going to summarise.' Chloe pulled back slightly, putting her hands on Livi's newly tension-free shoulders. 'You've been through a horrible time recently. I hope Matthew falls naked into a bed of nettles, but mostly I want you to feel better. You've missed out on a honeymoon, so take a free holiday on the French Riviera instead.'

'Going to Monaco wouldn't be a holiday. I'd be working.'

'Okay, but it would still be a change of scene. That can be just as useful to refresh your perspective on life. And yes, Xydis might be a love cheat, but if you don't need to write about that then just put it to the back of your mind and write about whatever he *does* want to talk about.' She gave a sly smile. 'Plus, you'd be doing me a favour. I could flat-sit.'

'What's wrong with your place?'

'My housemates are driving me crazy! Either I'm getting older or everyone else is getting louder, but since Mum and Dad moved to Devon, it's not like I can go and decompress with them for a couple of nights any more. Having a place to myself, even for ten days, would be bliss.'

'You know, you could always move in with me?' Livi suggested hopefully.

'Don't you only have one bedroom?'

'And a sofa-bed.' She made a face. 'Okay, that might not be ideal.'

'So if you go, can I stay? *Please?*' Chloe made pleading eyes. 'Just think of Xydis as a stepping stone to Erin. In fact…' She reached into a glass bowl on the table beside her and pulled out a small grey pebble. 'Here. Take this as a reminder.'

'That's a pretty small stepping stone.'

'It's symbolic. Then when you've finished the book, you can give it back because you won't need it any more.'

'That's actually kind of inspiring.' Livi took the pebble between her thumb and forefinger. 'You know, Xydis invited me to Spain to watch the race this weekend.'

'Are you kidding? That's amazing.' Chloe's eyebrows lifted all the way up to her hairline. 'Please tell me you're going.'

'I said I would, but you know…*this* weekend.'

'Ohhhh.' Chloe hugged her again. 'That sucks.'

'It really does.'

'But it could also be a good distraction?'

'Yeah…' She rested her head on her sister's shoulder and heaved another, even deeper sigh. Dario had said there was no need to make a decision until after the race, but she didn't want to wait that long. She had enough on her mind already. And everything Chloe had just said made sense. All she had to do was set her personal feelings about infidelity aside, focus on being impartial, and think of him solely as a means to an end, a way of getting to Erin and taking her career to the next level. After all, how hard could it be to grin—or grimace—and bear it for a few months?

'Fine.' She squeezed the pebble, now sitting warm and solid in her palm. 'I'll do it. You can use my flat and I'll think of him as a stepping stone. An extremely handsome, cheating stepping stone.'

'That's the spirit. Sort of.'

'And do you know what else?' She lifted her head again, filled with a new, empowering sense of resolve. 'I'll step all over him if I have to.'

'That's enough work commitments for the day,' Ethan commented, sliding into the back seat of a black sedan beside Dario. 'We just have one last thing to discuss.'

'Oh, yeah?' Dario leaned back against the headrest and closed his eyes as the car pulled away. After spending the latter part of the afternoon in a photoshoot for one of his team's sponsors, they were finally on their way to the airport. 'Go on.'

'Are you napping?'

'Napping *and* listening.'

'Uh-huh. I really think you should reconsider Ms Thorne.'

'This again?' Dario sighed heavily. 'I told you, I think she's perfect for the project.'

'Why? Because she's belligerent and obstructive?'

'Exactly. How many times have I been called those same things? I'd be a hypocrite to hold them against her.'

'So what, she's like your kindred spirit?'

'Something like that.' His lips quirked at the idea. 'Look, we need a writer quickly and she's good *and* available, so what's the problem? Aside from the fact that she clearly hates me.'

'No kidding. Any idea why?'

'I guess she believes what she reads in the press, but this book is supposed to be about changing people's perceptions of me, isn't it? So I figurc if I can persuade her, I can persuade anyone.'

'Is that all you want to do? Persuade her?' Ethan's tone was suspicious. 'Because she's pretty attractive for an ice queen.'

'I noticed.' Dario shrugged. Yes, she was attractive. *Very* attractive, in fact. As for being an ice queen… Honestly, it was a fairly accurate description, or it had been until he'd invited her to the race that weekend and her mask had slipped, revealing some kind of hidden pain beneath. *Intriguing*, that was the word he would have chosen for her. An intriguing, belligerent, incredibly sexy, yet surprisingly vulnerable librarian ice queen.

Not that it mattered. There were plenty of attractive women in the world and he had zero intention of getting distracted by any of them. Racing and relationships didn't mix, not for him anyway. It had taken almost a year for him to fully recover from the collapse of his marriage, but his driving had been better than ever since, and he wasn't about to mess up his chances at the World Championship again by getting involved with anyone else. If staying single was what it took to win, he was happy to do it.

'But if that's the reason you want her to write the book…?' Ethan went on.

'It's not.' He made an impatient sound. 'Don't worry. I'm one hundred percent committed to my career right now.'

'Good. Don't give her any more reasons to hate you or you'll ruin this book before it's even written. We don't want any more bad publicity. And by the way, what was that stuff about not wanting to talk about your marriage and divorce? I thought you said Karolina was okay with this project?'

'She is. I just think it's better to leave her out of it. I don't want any awkward questions.'

'Don't you think enough time has passed? I mean, you could probably tell the truth and the press would leave Karolina alone now.'

Dario opened his eyes to shoot his manager

a sceptical look. 'If you think that, you really don't know the press.'

'All I'm saying is that the truth would be a surefire way to rehabilitate your tarnished image.'

'I don't care.' Dario turned to look out of the window, fixing his gaze on some power lines by the side of the road. The 'truth', as Ethan called it, was a lot more complicated than that. 'It's private. Nobody else needs to know anything about it, least of all Livi Thorne.'

CHAPTER FOUR

'So, what do you think?' Kazia, Livi's own personal hospitality ambassador, asked as they wound their way along the crowded grid, looking at the cars lined up in the white painted boxes that marked their starting positions for the race. 'Pretty impressive, right?'

'Amazing,' Livi answered. It struck her as mind-blowing that they were standing in the spot where twenty of the best drivers in the world would be racing in less than half an hour. She didn't know much about motorsports, not yet anyway, despite her VIP lanyard, but she was already developing a newfound respect for the people involved. Logistically, the whole thing was incredible. The grid was so jam-packed, it was like fighting her way along Oxford Street on a Saturday lunchtime.

From what she could tell, there were three types of people. First and most obvious were the team members, dressed in brightly coloured liveries, gathered protectively around their cars. Second were the press, in smart casual sportswear, wielding cameras and microphones. Third and finally there were the glamorous people, in expensive designer outfits and impractical shoes, chatting and taking selfies like rich tourists. She had no idea which category she belonged in, but she was beginning to wish she'd dressed up in more than olive green wide-legged trousers, a white tank top and pink sandals.

After flying into Barcelona the previous evening, she'd spent the night in a five-star hotel in the Gothic quarter before a car had arrived after breakfast to escort her to the track. She hadn't spied either Dario or Ethan yet so there had been no chance to tell them her decision about the book, but she'd had a tour of the paddock and Dario's team's garage and motorhome, followed by lunch in the Paddock Club, where Kazia had shown her the trackside balcony where she could sit and sip cocktails during the race.

Despite her lack of enthusiasm for the project overall, she couldn't *not* get swept up in the racing atmosphere. Even the weather was playing along, gloriously sunny but with a refreshing breeze to blow away the smell of hot rubber. As cancelled wedding days went, she had to admit, this wasn't too bad. Definitely better than her original plan of lying under her duvet eating ice cream all day.

She took a deep, steadying breath at the thought of her cancelled wedding. She was fine, she reminded herself. Her emotions were under total control. Instead of the happiest day of her life, this was her first official day back at work, that was all. She was in a new country with a new mindset, and she intended to focus solely on research. In fact, that was her buzzword for the day: *research*. Definitely not wedding or bride or heartache or betrayal or…

'Is there anything else you'd like to see?' Kazia asked, mercifully disrupting her train of thought.

'I don't think so.' Livi shook her head. 'To be honest, I'm a little overwhelmed. I never imagined I'd get to see as much as this.'

'Dario said I should give you the full VIP treatment—and that was *before* he took pole in qualifying, so he wasn't just in a good mood.' Kazia's smile held a hint of mischief. 'So if you think of anything else, just let me know.'

'Thanks, but you've done plenty.' She smiled back. 'Unless there's any juicy gossip you'd like to share for my research notes?'

'About Dario? I wish.' To her surprise, Kazia laughed. 'I could tell you plenty about the rest of the team, but not him. He only has eyes for his car.' She gestured ahead. 'Look, there he is now. A lot of drivers prefer to keep off the grid when it's busy like this, but he likes to do a few last-minute checks with his race engineer.'

Livi followed the direction of Kazia's raised hand to where Dario was standing beside his car, talking intently to a woman with a clip-board. He was dressed in black and silver race overalls, although the top half was rolled down to his waist, revealing a tight white under-layer that served to accentuate the bulging muscles of his biceps and chest, especially when he stretched his arms over his head, like he was doing now, apparently in slow motion…

She pushed her sunglasses further up her nose as her mouth fell open, feeling a pulse of something in her chest, something warm and liquid that didn't feel quite as professional as she would have liked it to be. Even her blood seemed to be rushing a little bit faster, making her feel strangely light-headed.

Which was, of course, the moment he twisted in their direction and…

Phew! She jerked her head away and snapped her mouth shut, heaving a sigh of relief as a group of people stepped between them, blocking her view. What was the matter with her? She needed to get a grip, not stand there gawking like she'd never seen a man in tight clothing before.

She coughed, hoping her voice sounded something akin to normal. 'Well, I should probably get back to the Paddock Club.'

'Hang on.' Kazia was leaning to one side, looking past the group of people. 'I think Dario's waving us over.'

'He is?' She couldn't resist leaning too, surprised to find it was true. Dario was definitely beckoning in their direction. Which was…odd. The race was starting soon. Surely he had strategies to think about, visualisations to perform, overalls to pull up…her gaze drifted lower again…biceps to cover?

'Come on.' Kazia took hold of her arm, leading her purposefully through the crowd of people when her own feet refused to move.

'Livi, you made it.' Dario's smile widened as they approached. 'How was your journey?'

'The journey?' The warmth in his eyes was so unexpected it took her a couple of seconds to process the question, especially since her body seemed to be heating up again in response. 'Um…great, thank you. I've never travelled first class before. And all of this is amazing. Kazia's been taking good care of me.'

'Great. Thanks, Kaz.' He tossed a quick smile to her companion before turning back to her.

'So, do you have any questions for me? You know, for research purposes?'

'Oh…' She blinked, struggling to get her work head back on. Seriously, what was the matter with her? Surely she could think of *something*? 'Yes! Are you feeling confident?'

'Always.' He nodded firmly. 'There's no point in racing unless you believe you're capable of winning.'

'I guess not. What about coping with all this?' She gestured around the grid. 'I mean, there are so many people and cameras. It seems pretty intense.'

'You get used to it.' His expression was somewhere between a grin and a grimace. 'Although if you decide to write the book, I'll tell you how I *really* feel.'

'Well, actually…' She sucked in a breath, reaching a hand into her pocket to curl her fingers around the pebble Chloe had given her. *Just a stepping stone to Erin Cole*, she reminded herself, no matter how confusing she found him or how wildly her temperature seemed to be fluctuating right now. That was all he was, *just a stepping stone*. 'About the book…'

'Sorry to interrupt.' The woman with the clipboard stepped forward abruptly, one finger to her earpiece. 'Dario, it's time for the National Anthem.'

'Give me ten seconds.' He nodded, though he didn't take his gaze from Livi. 'Has Kazia shown you the team motorhome?'

'Yes.'

'How about I—'

'Pardon?' She winced as somebody shouted behind her, muffling the rest of his words.

'How about—' Somebody else shouted back.

'Sorry!' She gestured to the side of her head. 'I can't hear you.'

He moved closer, placing one hand lightly on her shoulder as he spoke straight into her ear. 'How about I meet you there after the race? Ethan's in the US on business, but we can still talk. I'll have to do media and a debrief, but I'll come and find you afterwards, okay?'

She tensed as his breath swept the side of her neck and his fingers skimmed the bare skin of her shoulder… It was only the lightest of touches and yet, just like when he'd taken her hand in Camille's office, she felt it like a physical shock.

'Um…' She had to force herself to exhale. 'Okay.'

'Dario.' The woman with the clipboard sounded impatient. 'You have to go *now*.'

'I'm going.' He rolled his eyes at Livi. 'Race days are a little hectic. Driving is the easy part.'

'I'll take your word for it.' She breathed a sigh of relief as he hurried away. 'Good luck!'

'That's so funny. He hardly ever talks to anyone before a race,' Kazia murmured as they watched him join the rest of the drivers gathered in front of a small orchestra. 'Now, it's almost two o'clock. We'd better get you settled.'

Livi made a noncommittal sound, distracted by a sudden aching sensation in her chest. Somehow, in all the commotion and excitement, she'd forgotten the race started at two, coincidentally the same time she'd been supposed to be getting married.

A lump rose in her throat. If Matthew had never met Sienna she would have been saying 'I do' in just a few short moments. Then, instead of watching twenty cars race around a track, she would have been in a barn in Sussex, dressed in a gorgeous duchesse satin gown, taking wedding photographs and celebrating with friends, eating wood-fired pizza and a strawberries and cream wedding cake before dancing with her new husband…

She pressed her lips together, ordering herself to stop spiralling, as she heard the strains of the National Anthem behind her. This wasn't the time or the place for an emotional breakdown. Maybe after the race she could allow herself a brief wallow about what-might-have-been, but right now she was absolutely *not* going to cry, no matter how hot and scratchy her eyes felt. The last thing she needed was to cause a scene around this many TV cameras.

Besides, there was no point in thinking about Matthew any longer. His role in her life was over. For the next few months she needed to focus all her attention and commitment on another man. On Dario Xydis, notorious love cheat.

It had been one of his better drives, Dario thought. Not perfect, but overall, the race had gone mostly to plan. There had been one minor incident on lap forty-two when he'd skidded off the track into the gravel, but after recapturing the lead with a late braking overtake on turn four, he'd kept it to the end, controlling the pace and finishing with a three-second lead on his teammate. Frankly, if that didn't impress Livi Thorne, nothing would.

For once, even his post-podium media commitments had gone well, without a single jibe or disagreement. He'd raced through them in record time before hurrying back to the motorhome for a quick shower and change of clothes, then headed straight to the debrief.

Unfortunately, that was when things had *stopped* working in his favour. His personal analysis of the race had been followed by that of Florent, the strategy director, whose graph-annotated speech seemed in no danger of ending any time soon.

A quick glance around the room suggested he wasn't the only one feeling restless. Several of the engineers were shuffling their feet, while the technical director had a hand over his mouth, attempting to stifle a yawn. Dario didn't blame him. The race was over, their strategy had been perfect and they'd won. What more was there to say?

Okay, he conceded, obviously there was a lot more to say. Part of the reason the team was so dominant this season was because Florent obsessed over the tiniest details, but the man needed to learn there was a time and a place for pit stop and race pace analysis, especially when people had their cute biographers to meet.

He peered surreptitiously at his phone. It had been almost three hours since he'd crossed the finish line. Would Livi still be waiting or would she have given up and left by now? He hoped the former—he was intrigued to find out what she'd made of the day—although keeping her waiting for three hours wasn't exactly the best way to persuade her to work for him. At this rate, he was going to end up with one of the journalists Ethan wanted.

Thankfully, it seemed that Werner, the team boss, was also growing impatient…

'That's great, Florent.' He put a hand on the strategy director's shoulder. 'But I think the rest can wait until we get back to HQ.'

'One more thing…'

'It can wait.' This time, Werner's tone was firmer. 'The team have done a great job today. Now it's time to celebrate.'

'I couldn't agree more.' Dario practically sprang out of his chair. 'I just have to meet someone first. Great job, everyone!'

He raced through the door before anyone could object, hurrying along the corridor and down the stairs of the motorhome to the chill-out area below. It was packed with team members and guests, but as far as he could see from a quick scan of the room, there was no sign of Livi.

Slowly, he wound his way through the crowd of people, accepting pats on the back and fist bumps on his way to the giant glass doors that led onto a terrace. There was a cordoned-off bar area out here, sheltered by a giant canopy, with a scattering of tables and a few tall plants for privacy. If she wasn't out here then he'd have to give up and accept that she'd probably gone back to her hotel, so he was relieved to see her sitting at a table in one corner, staring intently into a flute of champagne.

Relief shifted to disappointment as he took in her downturned mouth and slumped shoulders. So much for today convincing her to write his biography. She looked thoroughly miserable.

'Hey.' He put on a fake smile as he headed towards her. 'Sorry I took so long. I was afraid you might have left.'

She jerked her head up, her features instantly transforming into a neutral expression. 'It's okay. My flight isn't until tomorrow morning, so I have lots of time. Congratulations on your win.'

'I promised to get the race over with as quickly as possible, didn't I?' He sat down opposite, studying her up close for a moment before spreading his hands out in a gesture of defeat. She looked different, as if all the spark he'd admired the other day had completely faded away. 'So I guess this wasn't such a good idea, after all.'

'What do you mean?' Her brow knitted.

'I mean, a deal's a deal. I said I'd let you off the hook if you still didn't want to write my biography after the race and I meant it.'

She looked confused. 'I haven't said I don't want to write it.'

'Not out loud, but you look like you'd rather

be a million miles away.' He lifted his shoulders. 'Hey, if you didn't enjoy the race, that's fine. Motorsports aren't for everyone.'

'But I *did* enjoy it.'

He ducked his chin, fixing her with an incredulous look.

'I did!' she repeated. '*This...*' She waved a hand, as if she were drawing a circle in the air in front of her. 'This has nothing to do with that. I honestly enjoyed the race. It's just that I let myself start thinking about some other stuff afterwards and—' She stopped abruptly, biting her teeth into her bottom lip as it started to wobble.

'Livi?' He leaned forward in alarm.

'I'm sorry. It's nothing.'

'Don't be sorry.' He glanced sideways, subtly shaking his head as he noticed one of the team's media officers heading in their direction. Instantly, the man stopped and swerved away. 'Are you all right?'

There was a momentary pause before she sat up straighter, wrenching her shoulders back so violently it was amazing she didn't dislocate either of them. 'Absolutely. I've decided I *will* write the book. If you still want me to, that is?'

'I do.' He cocked an eyebrow. 'Although I have to admit I'm a little surprised. You were so against this project the other day, I figured

I only had a fifty-fifty shot of convincing you. Was the race that good?'

'It was a lot more exciting than I expected.' She cleared her throat. 'But mostly, I've just had a chance to think. It'll be a big change of pace, but I like a challenge.'

'Then welcome on board. So, how does this work? Do I lie down on a couch and pour out my life story while you make notes?'

'Not quite.' She looked relieved by the change in subject. 'I'll need to do some preliminary research before we discuss anything. Your manager has given me a lot of notes to work with, so I'll get started on those and then send you a list of any questions that come up. If you could record your answers and send them to me, that would be really helpful.'

'No problem.'

'Then by the time we meet in Monaco, I should know exactly which areas of your life to focus on.' Her lips curved slightly, revealing a tiny dimple at the left corner of her mouth. '*Then* you can lie on a couch and talk to me.'

'Sounds good.' He looked up as somebody appeared at the edge of his vision.

'Sorry to interrupt.' Kazia smiled between them. 'I just wanted to let Livi know, your car's ready when you are.'

'Thanks. I'm ready now.' Livi glanced back

at him. ‘Unless there’s anything else about the book you want to discuss?’

He hesitated, feeling strangely reluctant to let her go, but unable to think of a way to keep her there. ‘No, it sounds like you have it all under control.’

‘Then I’ll tell Camille to get the contract rolling.’

‘You know, you could stay,’ he couldn’t resist adding as she stood up. ‘There’ll be a party tonight, celebrating the win. You’re welcome to join us.’

‘Oh…’ A series of emotions seemed to flash over her face before she shook her head. ‘Thank you, but I don’t think so.’

‘Are you sure?’ He wasn’t sure why he was pushing this, only she’d looked so dejected before.

‘It wouldn’t really be appropriate, but I appreciate the offer.’ She gave him a half-speculative, half-suspicious look, as if she was trying to figure him out. ‘Congratulations again. See you in three weeks?’

‘Three weeks,’ he confirmed. ‘I’m looking forward to it.’

Oddly enough, he realised as she walked away, he meant it.

CHAPTER FIVE

Three weeks later

Wow.

Livi stepped onto the curved stone balcony of her hotel room and gave a small squeal of excitement. She'd managed to restrain herself when the porter had first opened the door of her suite, but it had been two minutes and she couldn't stay calm any longer. From here, she had a breathtaking view of Larvotto Beach, with its crystal-clear cobalt blue waters and even bluer sky. It was gorgeous, a lot like the suite itself, which was downright palatial, bigger than her entire flat back home and sumptuously decorated in a neutral palette of muted greens and soft, silvery greys. Everything about it was just… *Wow.*

'Is there anything else I can do for you, Miss Thorne?' the porter asked from behind her, possibly summoned by her squeal. 'Would you like some help unpacking?'

'No!' she answered quickly, horrified at the thought of him opening her suitcase and seeing her substantially less than designer wardrobe. 'Thanks, but I can manage.'

'As you wish. Mr Xydis says that he'll meet you in the restaurant at eight o'clock.'

'He does?' She drew her brows together. 'You mean, tonight?'

'Yes, although he also said he'd be happy to reschedule if it's inconvenient.'

'Oh…' She took a moment to consider. She hadn't honestly expected to see Dario today, but she supposed the sooner they got to work, the better. 'No, it's fine. Thank you.'

She handed him a ten-euro tip and then wandered slowly around the suite, smoothing her fingers over the faux sheepskin boucle armchair by the window and the mint green velvet sofa at the end of her queen-sized bed. And this was just the bedroom and living area. Next door was a separate study, complete with a dark wooden desk and cream leather chair, plus two more plush-looking sofas and a TV so large it was practically a cinema screen. There was even a crystal chandelier hanging from the ceiling. She'd expected the hotel to be luxurious but not *this* level of luxurious.

It would have been the perfect place for a honeymoon.

Her brows snapped together before she shook the thought away. Over the past three weeks she'd managed to stop thinking about Matthew every day and she had no intention of starting again now. If anything, this was a me-moon, a time to start appreciating her own company again…even if her days would be spent with Dario.

She kicked her shoes off and glanced at her watch. An eight o'clock dinner gave her three and a half hours to freshen up and relax. A four-hour delay at the airport meant that she'd arrived looking a lot less glamorous and a lot more sweaty and tired than she'd intended. She'd already been fairly exhausted after researching and writing like crazy over the past three weeks, as well as dealing with sympathy from her family and friends after her non-wedding day. As touched as she'd been by their concern, the effort of convincing everyone she was fine had been draining.

Thankfully, she genuinely *was* fine. Now the date had passed, her head was in a much better place. Thank goodness she'd managed to maintain a professional demeanour with Dario in Barcelona, just about anyway. He might have seemed friendly, genuine even, and yes, there had been one tremulous moment, but breaking down in tears would have undermined their professional relationship before it had even begun. Plus, his shoulder would have been the absolute worst she could have chosen to cry on!

Over the past few weeks of researching his life she'd learned more than enough about his womanising, even if, curiously, there had been a striking lack of any hard evidence. She hadn't found any kiss-and-tells, and most of the articles had been based on nothing more than gossip and hearsay from anonymous sources. Even in the photos she'd found of him with other women, he'd rarely had so much as an arm around them. There had been nothing massively incriminating, none of him holding hands with or kissing anyone other than his wife. If it hadn't been for his steadfast refusal to comment on, let alone deny the rumours surrounding his divorce, she might actually have given him the benefit of the doubt. Or she *would* have before Matthew had cheated on her. Now she knew just how well people could hide their dark secrets. Dario was probably just good at covering his tracks.

She deposited her sunhat and bag on the mirrored dressing table and headed for the bathroom. Like everything else in her suite, it was chic and luxurious, made of pale pink marble, with rose gold fittings and a large freestanding metallic tub. There was even a headrest in the bath, facing a one-way window looking out over the Mediterranean.

Enticing as that was, however, she needed to prioritise sleep if she was going to be even remotely alert tonight, so she made the tub a silent promise to be back very soon, then dipped into the shower instead, slathering herself in complimentary toiletries before slipping naked into her spacious new bed.

Bliss...

She let her eyelids drift closed as she lay back on the pillows. With a gentle breeze blowing in through the open balcony doors, she felt as though she were floating on a soft, feather-filled cloud. Absolute bliss…

Although… She opened her eyes again. She really ought to set an alarm, but her phone was still in her bag on the other side of the room and she was way too comfortable already to even contemplate getting up again. Shc supposed she could ring Reception and request a wake-up call using the phone on her bedside table, but how weird would that sound at this time in the afternoon? Besides, given how badly she was still sleeping in general, she doubted she'd be able to snooze for more than half an hour anyway. Surely she could risk a short nap?

The next thing she knew, there was a melodic chiming sound beside her head, rousing her back to consciousness.

Groggily, she lifted a hand, reaching for the hotel phone. ‘Hello?’

‘Hey.’ A deep Australian accent filled her ears. ‘Is everything okay?’

‘Yes. Why? Wha—’ She stopped, belatedly noticing the shadows around her. *Oh, no.* Her stomach lurched. Was she late? She was never late! ‘Is it eight already?’

‘It was.’ Thankfully, he sounded amused rather than annoyed. ‘About thirty minutes ago. I’ve been trying your mobile but there was no answer.’

‘I’m so sorry!’ She kicked at her sheets, wriggling her way off the bed. She must have left her mobile on airplane mode. ‘I overslept. Just give me five minutes to get dressed!’

‘Are you sure? If you’re tired we can meet tomorrow instead.’

‘No!’ She refused to be so unprofessional. ‘You’re already here. Just stay where you are and I won’t be long.’

She dropped the phone and sprinted towards her suitcase, wrestling with the zip for thirty seconds before flinging it open and pulling on some clean underwear and one of the several black dresses she’d brought for work. Then she slipped her feet into a pair of black ballet pumps, grabbed her tote and hurtled towards the door.

A sidelong glance in the mirror brought her to an appalled halt. Her sleeveless shift gave off a suitably smart and efficient vibe, but sleeping on wet hair had been a *really* bad idea. There were tufts sticking out all over the place, some of them practically vertical. It looked like she'd just suffered a minor electrical shock.

Quickly, she smoothed her hands over her head. She could fix this, she told herself, or at least do some damage control. All she needed was a hairband, some mousse and a lot of vigorous brushing.

Thirty seconds later, she was on her way again, her blonde hair now twisted into a severe-looking bun as she exited the lift and walked briskly across the lobby towards the terrace restaurant.

'Hi.' She stopped in front of the maître d', pausing briefly to catch her breath. 'I'm here to meet Dario Xydis.'

'Of course.' The man inclined his head as if he was perfectly accustomed to women panting heavily in front of him. 'He's this way.'

'Thank you.'

She lifted her chin in the air, trying to project an air of calm confidence as he led her around the edge of a large kidney-shaped swimming pool, past several discreetly spaced-out diners, towards a candlelit table set beneath an olive tree canopy on the far side.

Dario stood up as they approached. In contrast to her, he was dressed casually in white trousers and a pale blue shirt with the top couple of buttons undone, and with a layer of light stubble across his jaw he looked even more strikingly handsome than she'd remembered.

Damn. A strange, sharp thrill rippled through her, settling in the pit of her stomach.

'I'm sorry I woke you.' He took a step forward, looking as though he was about to kiss her cheek before changing his mind and pulling out a wooden chair instead. 'You must have been tired.'

'Yes.' She slipped onto the white seat cushion, waiting until he'd pulled his hands away again before leaning back against the frame. 'But I only meant to nap. It's so strange for me to sleep more than a couple of hours.'

'Comfortable bed?'

'Comfortable everything. This hotel is spectacular.'

'I'm glad you like it.'

'I think it would be impossible not to.' She smiled tightly. 'You didn't have to book anything so luxurious, but I can't say I object either. Thank you.'

'You're welcome. By the way, I hope you don't mind, but I ordered us some drinks.' He lifted a hand and almost immediately, a waiter appeared bearing two glasses on a tray. 'I thought champagne cocktails to celebrate your arrival?'

'Sounds perfect.'

'To a successful collaboration.' He lifted his glass in the air, dark eyes dancing.

'A successful collaboration,' she echoed, taking a sip and casting a surreptitious look around the terrace at the same time. Now that her panic about being late was over, she couldn't help but notice how glamorous everyone else on the terrace looked. Meanwhile, she'd rushed out of her suite without even putting on make-up. She probably stuck out like a sore thumb. If it wasn't for Dario, she doubted she would have been allowed in.

Not that her appearance mattered, she reminded herself sternly. She was there to work, not to dress up. And she *definitely* didn't care about impressing Dario, no matter how attractive or charming or sexy he… *No!* She threw a mental wall up, stopping the thought in its tracks. He was attractive, objectively speaking, but charming and sexy? Absolutely not. She refused to be charmed by a cheater. As for finding him sexy? Not if her inner voice had anything to do with it.

'So…' She put her glass down, deciding to get

straight to business. ‘Thank you for answering my preliminary questions so promptly. Your voice notes were very helpful. I presume you’ve seen the plan for the book?’

‘Yes. Ethan tells me you have a draft already.’

‘An *extremely* rough one. Definitely not publishable, but it’s useful to have a structure. I want the book to start at the end of the story, with whatever happens in the Championship this year, then go back to the start so the reader can follow your journey to that point.’

‘Whatever you think is best.’ He gave a slow smile. ‘I’m in your hands.’

‘Right.’ She pursed her lips, firmly rejecting the mental image that comment evoked. ‘Unfortunately, it’s a little tricky with the Championship still ongoing. Given the size of your lead, I’m writing under the presumption you’ll win, but I also think it’s important for us to discuss both scenarios. That way I can cover either.’ She looked at him expectantly. ‘So, let’s say you win. How will you feel?’

‘Like I’ve achieved my life’s dream.’

‘And if you don’t?’

He grimaced. ‘Honestly, I don’t let myself think about that. Keeping a positive mental attitude is important.’

‘But—’

‘Let’s just say that if I lose, you can write

whatever you want.' He gestured towards the menu. 'Now, what would you like to eat? They do a great filet mignon here.'

'That sounds good.' She gave a curt nod. 'However, I'd also like to discuss—'

'Maybe we should leave the work talk for tonight?' he interrupted. 'You've only just arrived. Why not consider this a welcome to Monaco dinner?'

'*Leave* the work talk?' She lifted an eyebrow. 'I thought you invited me here to work?'

'Yes, but surely we can enjoy a friendly dinner as well?'

'No.' She was pleased with how definite she sounded. 'As your biographer, it's important for me to maintain a professional distance. I'm not here to be *friendly*.'

'Okay.' His gaze flicked upwards at the waiter who had silently appeared beside the table. 'The filet mignon for both of us, please. Rare for me and...?' He turned enquiringly towards her.

'Oh...' She looked to the waiter, his expression a blank mask though it would have been impossible for him not to overhear her last words. 'Um, medium rare, thank you.' She waited until he was gone before clearing her throat awkwardly. 'As I was saying, this is a business meeting.'

'If that's what you want,' he agreed, although

something about his expression struck her as faintly disappointed. 'What would you like to discuss?'

'First off, logistics. I suggest that we meet twice a day, morning and afternoon. Say nine until twelve and two until four? Then I'll have plenty of time to work on my notes around that.'

'No problem. I'll be away in Genoa for a wedding one day, otherwise I'm all yours.'

'Good. Then there's the question of a venue. I have an office in my suite, or I could ask the hotel if they have a meeting room we could use?'

'Fine with me, although your agent said you'd prefer to meet in my apartment?'

'Oh…yes.' She took another sip of champagne, stalling for time while she tried to come up with some excuse. It was true that she usually conducted interviews in her subjects' homes. She found it useful, since being in somebody else's personal space provided valuable insights into their personality. Unfortunately, it also created a sense of intimacy, something she really wanted to avoid with Dario.

She put her glass down again. 'I wouldn't want to inconvenience you.'

'It's no inconvenience. It's partly why I chose this hotel. My apartment is only a five-minute walk away.'

'Okay. Great.' She gritted her teeth. 'If you

message me the address, I'll come to you tomorrow.'

'I'll have coffee ready. How do you like it?'

'Whatever you have is fine.' She kept her tone brisk. 'Next, there's the matter of recordings. Are you happy for me to record our conversations? They'll be for my use only, in case I need to refer back to anything, and I'll delete everything after the book is approved, you have my word.'

'Go ahead.' He nodded. 'It must be a lot of work, researching a complete stranger and turning their life into a book.'

'It is.'

'I wouldn't know where to begin.'

She unclenched her jaw slightly. 'Everyone's process is different, but it helps me to think of a biography as a huge jigsaw puzzle. My job is to take all of your formative moments and milestones and arrange them in a way that's clear and compelling and hopefully thought-provoking, too.'

'Thought-provoking?' He laughed softly. 'I've never been called that before.'

'But you are. Everyone is.' She leaned forward, warming to her theme. 'Personally, I think the best biographies are about more than a single person. We all need a context, right? So there are bigger themes and questions to investigate. In your case, what makes a person want to do extreme sports? What levels of physical and mental toughness are required to be successful? Ultimately, what are the qualities that make a world champion? Then there are the personal elements that people relate to—you know, the struggles and adversities.'

'I didn't realise just how much work you're being expected to do in a short time.' His gaze moved over her face. 'It's impressive.'

She felt a flush of warmth at the compliment, although if he thought he could charm her, he could think again…even if the way he was looking at her was making it a little harder to breathe.

'I guess we all have our strengths. I wouldn't know how to race cars either.' She exhaled shakily before reaching into her tote and extracting a small notepad and pen. 'So, I just have a little basic fact checking to do, if that's all right?'

'Sure.' His head tilted. 'You don't relax, do you?'

'Not when I'm working.' She gave him a pointed look. 'Do you relax when you're driving?'

'Touché.' He leaned back in his chair, folding one long leg over the other. 'Okay then. Ask away.'

CHAPTER SIX

'HEY, XYDIS! We need to talk about Belgium.'

Dario stopped in the lobby of his apartment building. He'd been up before dawn, cycling up into the mountain passes before the sun got too high, wanting to stretch his legs and clear his head before Livi arrived for their first day of interviews. He hadn't anticipated coming face to face with a fierce-looking Javier Varela, the Argentinian driver he'd almost clashed tyres with during their last race, who was coincidentally also the driver who lived in the apartment two floors below his…

'I have nothing to say about Belgium.' He planted his feet wide apart.

'Oh yeah?' Javier advanced slowly, amber eyes narrowed. 'How about we go outside and I make you?'

'How about you try it right here?'

'If that's what you want.'

'I can do this wherever you like.'

There was a tense five-second silence while they eyeballed each other before both dissolving into laughter at the same moment.

'You know, as much as I'd love to pummel you, I have a tennis match in a quarter of an hour.' Javier clapped a hand on Dario's shoulder. 'How about we reschedule?'

'Any time.' Dario grinned. 'Or you could just come by for a drink later?'

'Even better.' Javier started past him and then stopped. 'Hey, why don't you come and play doubles now? I could call one of the other guys.'

'That sounds fun, but I've got to work on this biography project.'

'Wow, I wish I was old enough for a biography.' Javier smirked. 'Good luck.'

Dario raised a hand before heading to the stairwell, shunning the lift in favour of the seven flights of steps it took to reach his apartment. Once there, he kicked his trainers off in the hallway, chugged a mango and almond milk protein shake from the fridge, and then looked appraisingly around the open-plan living area.

What would Livi think of his home? he wondered. Personally, he liked this space, with its two white curved sofas set around a circular oak coffee table in the centre, with a pale grey fireplace wall on one side—behind which lay his slightly less minimalist man-cave—and glass doors opening onto a large plant-filled balcony on the other, but it wasn't as if he spent much time or energy on decor.

Not that it mattered what she thought, he reminded himself. He didn't need to impress her; he only needed to work with her. This year was about winning the Championship and silencing his critics, not getting distracted, especially by a woman he'd only recently met, no matter how intriguing or attractive he found her. Careerwise, he was on a roll. This season was his best shot at the Championship, his ultimate life goal, and he wasn't about to risk messing it up again. His career had flourished since he'd been single; he needed to remember that.

Thankfully, Livi's ice queen demeanour was making it easy. Last night was definitely the last time he was inviting her to dinner. The food had been excellent, but the rest of the evening had been excruciating. Kind of disappointing too. He'd assumed that she'd relax a little once she arrived but, just like in Barcelona, she'd been determined to keep the conversation focused solely on work. Hell, she'd even been dressed for a board meeting!

Maybe it was just her professional persona, but he'd had the feeling she'd been making a point too, that she wasn't there to enjoy herself, and that she wouldn't with him anyway. He didn't know if it was because of his bad reputation or if he was simply losing his touch with the opposite sex, but overall, it had felt a little insulting. Honestly, he'd been relieved when the evening had come to an end, with her finally closing her notebook and declaring she wanted an early night.

He was just stepping out of the shower, rubbing a towel through his wet hair, when his intercom buzzed.

'There's a Ms Livi Thorne to see you,' his doorman informed him when he answered.

'Thanks, Jules. Send her up.'

He went through to the kitchen, flicking on his espresso maker and then leaving the front door open as he went into his bedroom and quickly pulled on a white crew neck T-shirt and a pair of black chino shorts.

'Am I early?' Livi was already waiting when he came back, one kitten-heeled shoe in his apartment, the other still in the corridor, as if she hadn't fully decided whether or not to enter. Her hair was tied back as usual and she was wearing a knee-length black dress almost identical to the one she'd worn last night, aside from a row of silver buttons, with a matching blazer slung over one arm and a weathered-looking leather satchel on the other.

'You're right on time.' He gave her a welcoming smile despite his misgivings, ushering her inside and closing the door. 'Come on in.'

'Thank you.' She took a few steps into the kitchen and looked around. 'This is nice.'

'You sound surprised.'

'No… Well, maybe a little.' She looked mildly embarrassed. 'I wasn't sure what to expect. I've never been in the home of a world-famous racing driver before.'

'Gold lacquer? Or maybe a wall of trophies with a robot butler to polish them?'

'Possibly.'

'Too bad I gave him the day off to recharge.' He grinned and clapped his hands together. 'Can I make you an espresso before we start? I'm having one.'

'No, thanks. I've just had breakfast on my balcony.'

'All right, then.' He led her through to the living area. 'Make yourself comfortable.'

Two minutes later, he came back to find her sitting on the sofa facing the window, both hands clasped around one knee, with a laptop, notepad and selection of stationery arranged neatly on the coffee table.

'This looks serious.' He sat on the opposite sofa.

'It is.' She sat forward to press a button on her phone. 'Starting voice recording now.'

'No small talk?' He took a sip of coffee.

'I think it's best to dive straight in.' She reached for her notepad and crossed her legs at the ankles. Nice ankles, he noticed, neat and shapely, like the rest of her legs…

'I thought we'd start by talking about your family. Your parents emigrated from Greece soon after you were born, is that right?'

'Yes.' He coughed, trying to clear the sudden huskiness in his throat as he tamped down the urge to look at her legs again. 'They opened a bakery in Sydney.'

'That must have been hard work?'

'It meant a lot of early mornings and long hours. They gave me a strong work ethic.'

'Did you ever think of following in their footsteps?' She pulled a pen out from behind her head, as if she'd had it tucked away in her bun. 'You're the eldest. Didn't they want you to take over the business?'

'If they did, they never mentioned it.' He shifted position, wondering what that hair would look like down, how it would feel if he drew his fingers through it… 'As for me, I make a pretty decent *karydopita*, but no, I never considered it.'

She squirmed slightly, as if she was trying to get comfortable. 'Why not?'

'Because once I tried karting there was nothing else I wanted to do with my life.'

She nodded, jotting something down. 'Do you remember the first time?'

'Vividly. It was at a friend's birthday party when I was seven years old. I fell in love with driving straight away.'

'Fell in love?' Her pen paused, though she didn't look up.

'Head over heels.' He smiled at the memory. 'Maybe the adrenaline rush had something to do with it, but it felt natural too. Instinctive. Like the car was an extension of me.'

'When did you know you wanted it to be your career?'

'Pretty much the same moment.'

'And how did your parents feel about that? Were they supportive?'

'Completely. Once they realised how much I loved driving, they did everything they could to support me.'

She nodded slowly, her gaze still fixed on her notepad. 'Karting is quite expensive though, isn't it?'

'Extremely.' He made a face. 'Although, I'm ashamed to admit, I didn't think much about that to begin with. I was probably ten or eleven before I realised how much it cost them, not just in money, but in time, too: taking me to races, standing around, watching me go round and round. It had to be pretty boring for them.'

'What about your sisters? You have two, don't you? Did they enjoy karting as well?'

'Definitely not. Zoe tried it for a while, but she was never obsessed like me, and Elena was more into art.' He spread his arms out, stretching them over the back of the sofa. 'It caused some issues between us for a while, especially since they were the ones helping out in the shop while I went racing. I remember complaining about how tired I was after a track day one time. They both told me I was selfish.'

'How did you feel about that?'

'Not very happy. I think I stomped up to my room and sulked for a couple of hours, until I realised they were right. That's when I realised I either had to give up racing or become the best in the world.' He chuckled. 'And maybe do a few more shifts in the bakery.'

She ignored the joke. 'So you decided to become the best? That's a lot of pressure to put on yourself.'

'It was the only way to justify what I was doing. Luckily, it worked out.'

'And how is your relationship with your sisters now?'

'Pretty good. I made sure to pay them back once I started making decent money. College tuition, houses, weddings, all that kind of stuff.

They're both married and have kids now. Zoe is a teacher and Elena is a graphic designer.'

'What about your parents? What are they doing?'

'They're happily retired in Palm Beach, just north of Sydney.'

'So, family-wise, everything's fine?'

'Yes. My family are great. We're very close.'

'Huh.' Her brow creased slightly, as if she found it hard to believe. 'So, going back to your teenage years. How was school? Did karting have any effect on your grades?'

He drained his espresso cup, wondering why she now seemed so determined to avoid eye contact. She hadn't had a problem looking at him last night. Presumably it was some kind of professional trick to encourage him to talk freely and forget she was there. As if that was likely with those legs…

He put his cup down again. 'To be honest, I was never much of a student. Although I would probably have hated school whether or not I was good at it.'

'Why?'

'Growing up, I was short for my age and some kids made fun of me. I got into a lot of fights.'

'Fights?' She looked up finally, tapping the end of her pen against her bottom lip.

'Yes. I never went looking for them, but when

somebody insults me, I insult them back.' His gaze dropped to her mouth before he wrenched it back up again. 'I've never been good at walking away from confrontation.'

'Maybe you should give it a try? Then you wouldn't need a biography to improve your reputation.' She held his gaze this time, a hint of challenge in hers. 'That's part of your problem with the media, isn't it?'

'Maybe I should, but driving is intense. When I finish a race, I'm usually exhausted. Having to deal with digs and criticisms from the press afterwards can be wearing. I'd like to see any of them do what I do and still keep their temper.'

'Surely you've had media training?'

He felt a flash of irritation. Yes, he'd had plenty of media training. Before the collapse of his marriage, he'd been reasonably good at following it, too. It was only when his personal life had become all anyone would ask him about that he'd found his temper fraying. Now there were days when he felt as if he was at war with the media, facing questions shaped deliberately to make him react, to get a soundbite or meme out of him…

Unfortunately, he was beginning to think that she was just like them. He'd assumed this book would be all facts and figures and descriptions of his races, not some kind of humourless deep dive into his psyche. She might be good at her job, but maybe he'd made a mistake and he ought to have hired one of the journalists Ethan had recommended. Or maybe the person who'd recommended her had been playing a twisted joke at his expense…

The sinking feeling in his stomach told him this was going to be a long ten days.

'Dario?' She was arching an eyebrow at him.

'Like I said, I've never been good at walking away.'

'Okay, moving on…' Her lips pursed briefly. 'How do you think your parents feel about your career now? Are they proud?'

'I hope so, although my mother thinks I've driven enough. She keeps suggesting I should retire and give her some grandchildren.'

'But that's not what you want?'

'They say you lose a second per lap for every child.'

Her head snapped up. 'Excuse me?'

'When you're racing, losing concentration for even a fraction of a second can be the difference between coming first and last. Success requires one hundred percent commitment and focus.'

'In other words, driving comes before anything else?'

'Yes. It may sound selfish, but it's a question of priorities.'

'What about relationships?' She lifted her eyes to the ceiling when he folded his arms. 'I mean, *in general*. I'm not asking about your marriage.'

He clenched his jaw for a couple of seconds before conceding the point. 'Fair enough. Relationships and sports are tough. I've come to realise that I can only be successful at one, not both.'

'Plenty of sportspeople have happy relationships.'

'Good for them.'

'So you're not in a serious relationship right now?'

'I'm not in any kind of relationship right now.'

'There's no one at all?'

'No.' He frowned at her sceptical expression. 'Is that so hard to believe?'

'It's just that you have, or *had*, a…reputation.'

'So I've heard.'

'All right, but given how many women your name has been linked to in the past, being single must be quite a change?'

He felt his eyes narrow. 'If you say so.'

A hint of pink crept into her cheeks in response. 'In other words, you're suggesting a healthy relationship and a driving career are incompatible?'

'Yes. Not for everyone, but definitely for me.'

'Why?' She looked baffled.

'I have to travel a lot, and when I'm not travelling, I'm training. There isn't much time for relationships.'

'Other drivers seem to manage.'

'Like I said, good for them. Maybe I just train harder.'

'It sounds lonely.'

'Sometimes, perhaps, but my track record at relationships is pretty abysmal. Staying single is for the best, especially if I want to win the World Championship.'

He sat back in his chair and folded his arms, indicating he didn't wish to discuss the subject any further, although he'd spent a lot of time thinking about it after his divorce. It wasn't that he hadn't cared about Karolina, or any of his past girlfriends, for that matter, but his career demanded a certain degree of narcissism. He'd certainly never meant to hurt any of his exes, or make them feel any less than special, and yet he'd always seemed to do it anyway. Then things had inevitably gone wrong and, ironically, he'd lost the very focus they'd accused him of putting before everything else.

It wasn't a situation he intended to place himself in again. If it hadn't been for the collapse of his marriage, he could have been a world champion already, and he doubted his career could withstand another ruined season. His sponsors would drop him and then the team would start looking elsewhere for a driver. None of which he intended to tell his biographer. She could put travel and training in the book and leave it at that.

Unfortunately, it seemed that she wasn't going to let him off the hook so easily.

'Why "especially"? Do you really think a relationship would ruin your chance to be a world champion?' Livi was staring hard at him now.

'Not necessarily, but...potentially.' He was aware of a muscle pulsing in his jaw. Obviously, he'd given away more than he'd intended, since their conversation was veering dangerously close to what had happened two years ago. 'It's too big a risk to take.'

She dug her teeth into her bottom lip, as if she was biting back a different question to the one she eventually asked. 'So would you describe yourself as a workaholic?'

'No,' he answered firmly. 'That word suggests a problem, like an addiction, but I love what I do. There's nothing wrong with that, is there?'

'I don't think so.' She looked thoughtful. 'Although some people might disagree.'

He leaned forward, bracing his forearms

across his knees. 'Then maybe they're in the wrong jobs?'

'Hmm.' She gave a low murmur, refusing to engage. 'So, tell me about the rest of your family…'

This was going to be harder than she'd thought.

Livi collapsed onto the swing-sofa on her balcony, curling her bare feet beneath her as she tried to process her first day of interviewing Dario. Work-wise, it had been reasonably productive. He'd been a little defensive about certain subjects, but overall she'd been impressed by his forthright manner and matter-of-fact answers. The impression he gave was of somebody who knew who he was, who knew his strengths and weaknesses and was happy in his own skin. Laid-back and unpretentious, just like his apartment.

It was exactly the opposite of what she'd hoped.

She stretched her arms over her head, releasing her hair from the tight bun she'd worn all day. It wasn't that she'd *wanted* him to be difficult. On the contrary, there was nothing worse than a subject who refused to engage properly with questions, but self-awareness like his was far too attractive a quality, and the absolute last thing she needed was to find herself any more drawn to him.

As much as she hated the admission, it was impossible to keep on denying his obvious sex appeal. When he'd met her in the hallway, barefoot and still damp from a shower, with a T-shirt clinging to his abs in a way that was almost indecent, it had been all she could do not to throw herself at him.

She only hoped that she'd managed to project an outwardly calm demeanour because her insides had been anything but. She'd been intensely aware of him throughout their whole interview, and not in a professional way. It had been a completely physical awareness, her nerves alert to every small movement he'd made. To her horror, she'd even found herself mirroring them, until she'd realised and focused her attention firmly on her notepad. Then she'd had to keep her eyes averted most of the time, just to avoid being distracted by those full, sensual lips and mesmerising cheekbones.

Even his smell had been distracting! Every time he'd shifted position, she'd felt as if her nostrils were being assailed by a wave of pheromones, sending quivers of sensation rippling through her body. Obviously, it was just chemistry, an inconvenient biological response based solely on hormones—certainly with no deeper meaning—but it had been *so* frustrating, as if her own body was working against her.

She kneaded her fingers into her shoulders, willing her body to relax now that her first day was finally over, but it was like massaging a brick. Chloe would be appalled.

Frankly, it was a little mortifying that a man she despised could be having such a powerful physical effect on her, and so soon after her cancelled wedding, too! Even if, theoretically, she didn't despise him—which she did!—she was absolutely *not* interested in any kind of relationship right now—and nor was he, judging by what he'd told her.

As for some kind of rebound fling, a purely physical liaison…that was totally out of the question. Dislike aside, there was absolutely no way she could rebound with a man like Dario Xydis. For one thing, because he was her subject, for another, because it would be too, *too* ironic to rebound with a renowned womaniser. Besides, even if he *was* single—a fact she still found hard to believe, no matter what he said—it wasn't as if a man like him would ever look twice at a woman like her, one who hadn't been 'physical' enough for her own fiancé.

Although… She glanced down at her ankles. She thought she'd noticed Dario looking at them earlier. It had been a swift glance, no more than a couple of seconds, and yet the heat in his gaze seemed to have seared into her skin like a brand, penetrating right to her core. She hadn't felt heat like that for a long time, as if her insides had been frozen and she hadn't even been aware of the fact. Maybe she wasn't as unattractive as Matthew had made her feel. Maybe she hadn't even been the problem. It wasn't as if he'd been so exciting in bed…

What would Dario be like? The thought entered her mind before she could block it, accompanied by images of them both naked, limbs tangled together, skin covered in a sheen of sweat, his lips on her throat as she trailed her fingers down his back, drawing him closer… Would he take his time or be more perfunctory like Matthew? Would he care as much about her own pleasure as his own?

A kaleidoscope of butterflies erupted in her stomach, robbing her of breath for a few seconds. This was exactly the kind of thing she *shouldn't* be thinking! She was letting her imagination run away with her and she needed to get a grip fast—and she would. The first day of a new job was often the hardest, after all. Now that she knew what to expect, she could get her hormones under control, armour herself against the onslaught of Dario's charisma, and focus all her attention on writing the book. It was like he'd said, success required one hundred percent commitment, and that was what she needed to give this project if she was going to get Erin Cole's attention. Her only relationship for the foreseeable future would be with her career.

She sank back against the swing cushions, trying to ignore the rash of goosebumps skittering across her skin. This was *definitely* going to be harder than she'd thought.

CHAPTER SEVEN

SHE'D BEEN OVERREACTING, Livi decided, Erin Cole's Greatest Hits album blasting through her AirPods as she ran along Port Hercule towards the Casino de Monte-Carlo the following morning, acclimatising herself to her new surroundings. There were so many yachts and cruise ships moored here she'd given up counting, but the views were still jaw-dropping, even more than she'd anticipated. The sheer cliffs that surrounded the harbour seemed to trap the early morning sun, reflecting it back off the hundreds of high-rise buildings onto the Mediterranean Sea below, making the whole world seem to shimmer and sparkle.

She'd brought her running gear with her on impulse, although she hadn't worn it in forever—or at least since the day of Matthew's bombshell—and it was becoming painfully obvious that her body was severely out of practice. As hard as she was trying to control her breathing and rhythm, her heart was beginning to feel like it wanted to push its way out of her chest, though on the plus side, at least she wasn't thinking about Dario—not until now anyway.

Urgh. In her brain's defence, however, his intrusion into her thoughts was probably due to the fact that she'd spent most of the previous evening watching YouTube clips of his old races. According to most commentators, he was both technically brilliant and inherently talented, too, with an ability to make seemingly impossible overtakes look easy. There had been one memorable instance in Baku three years ago, where he'd seemed to be aiming for the outside of a corner, then braked early and swung to the left, dive-bombing up the inside. Then there had been another overtake in Mexico last year, where he'd driven up the inside of a tight corner alongside another car, braking so late that they'd almost touched wheels, yet somehow held his nerve, forcing the other driver off the racing line so he could take the lead. There had also been several occasions when he'd overtaken two cars at once. His ability to corner at speeds of up to two hundred miles an hour, despite the powerful G-forces, struck her as mind-blowing.

The collapse in his form two years ago had looked even worse by comparison. She was no expert, but even she had been able to see that he'd been driving like a rookie, not an experienced racer. He'd misjudged his tyre grip in rainy conditions, overshot braking points repeatedly, and locked up at times when he ought to have been in control. His attempts at overtakes had been sloppy and he'd even driven into the wall in Singapore. She hadn't expected to feel sorry for him, and yet she had.

And why was she *still* thinking about him?

Fortunately, her phone chose that moment to ring, bringing her to a halt beside a particularly lavish multi-decked superyacht.

'Hello?'

'Hey!' Chloe sounded in a good mood. 'How's it going? Tell me everything!'

'Pretty well, I think.' She bent over, resting her hands on her thighs as she struggled to get her breath back. 'But you know, it's only been one day.'

'Did you get any deep, dark secrets out of him yet?'

'No.'

'Nothing at all?'

'Chloe…'

'Yeah, yeah, you couldn't tell me even if you had. Spoilsport. Why are you so breathless, by the way?'

'I'm running.'

'You're exercising again? That's great!'

'You wouldn't say that if you could see me. I'm so out of shape, it's embarrassing.'

'You'll bounce back, don't worry. Just stay hydrated and remember to cool down properly.' Chloe's tone turned brisk. 'So, I'm calling because I have some news.'

'Good or bad?' She arched her back. 'Please don't tell me you've burned down my flat.'

'Not yet, but I *did* have a visitor last night.' Chloe paused for effect. 'A certain ex-fiancé of somebody.'

'Matthew?' Livi jumped as if he'd just materialised in front of her. 'What did he want?'

'He came to collect a box of stuff. It was tucked away in the corner of his old wardrobe, so I figured it was okay to let him take it.'

'Oh. Yeah, it's fine, don't worry.' She pressed a hand to her forehead. 'How did he seem?'

'Well, he was pretty shocked when I just *happened* to mention that you were in Monaco with a gorgeous millionaire.' Chloe sounded gleeful. 'I told you he'd find out somehow.'

'You didn't!' Livi gasped.

'Of course I did. I might even have suggested it was a romantic getaway. His jaw practically fell off. I wish I had a picture to send you.'

'Actually, that would have been great.' Livi laughed. 'Thank you.'

'Any time. Look, I'd better get to work, but enjoy your holiday!'

'It's not a—' She rolled her eyes as Chloe hung up, then glanced at her watch. She should probably start thinking about work now too. There was still an hour before she needed to meet Dario, but she wanted a shower and some breakfast first.

She swung around, concentrating on her breathing as she put one foot in front of the other, gradually increasing her pace.

There... She felt a rush of endorphin-fuelled elation, boosted by Chloe's news. She was in total control—of her body, her mind *and* her emotions. This was good. This was progress. This was…painful?

Ow! She staggered as a tight, burning sensation shot up her right leg. Quickly, she hopped onto her other foot, trying to stave off the cramp, but it was too late. Her calf muscles were already going into spasm…

Ow, ow, ow!

She gave up trying to run through the pain, collapsing onto the pavement and clutching at her leg instead. Fortunately, there was nobody else on this stretch of pavement right now to see her. The only possible witnesses were the super-rich people on their yachts and they were probably too busy reading about stock markets over breakfast to pay her any attention.

Carefully, she pulled her foot towards her, sucking air through her teeth as she tried to stretch out the muscle, but the burning sensation refused to ease. There was nothing to do but sit here, wait it out and hope that nobody…

'Livi?'

She stiffened, her muscles tightening even more as she looked up to see Dario veer off the road on a racing bicycle and come riding towards her, dressed in grey shorts and a black vest top.

'Oh…hi.' She pulled her AirPods out and made a misguided, quickly abandoned attempt to stand up before sinking back down onto the pavement, scrunching her face up with a combination of pain and mortification.

'Hey.' He dismounted, removing his helmet and leaning his bike against a conveniently placed palm tree before hurrying over to crouch in front of her. 'Are you okay?'

'Yes.' She inhaled sharply as the scent of fresh sweat and musky male filled her nostrils, giving a terse nod that turned into a shake of the head. 'No. Cramp.'

'Ah.' He looked sympathetic, gesturing to her leg. 'May I?'

She hesitated for a nanosecond before nodding again. Considering how conflicted she felt around him, physical contact struck her as a supremely bad idea, but the pain was so bad, anything had to be better than just sitting there.

'Okay, here we go.' He wrapped his hands around her calf, digging his thumbs deep into the muscle and moving them in small circles. 'Try to breathe normally.'

'I'm trying.' She winced. 'It's just really bad.'

Although now that she said it, the pain was already receding, melting away beneath his fingertips. They felt so good, pressing into her skin with a firm but gentle pressure…and she really needed to stop ogling his biceps, even though they were right in her eye-line, thick and glistening with sweat, like they were actually coated in oil… A wave of heat surged through her, like she'd just stepped into a sauna.

'Yes, keep doing that.' She tipped her head back, stifling a whimper. 'You must have magic thumbs.'

'I do my best.' He slowed down the rhythm. 'How does that feel?'

'*Much* better.'

'Good.' He laid her leg down gently on the pavement. 'Now don't move. You need to rest the muscle for a while.'

She jerked her head upright again. 'I can't just sit here.'

'Why not?'

She gestured towards the yachts. 'The billionaires might send someone to shoo me off with an oar or something.'

'Then they can shoo us both.'

'What are you—' She did a double take as he sat down beside her. 'Oh, no, you don't have to stay. I'll just give it a few minutes before heading back to the hotel. I'm sure I'll be fine.'

'Probably.' He rubbed a hand over his chin. 'Although I'm not sure that would read very well in the book. I'd hate to come across as the kind of man who abandons a damsel in distress.'

'What if I promise to leave that part out?'

'See you in forty-five minutes for work then?' He chuckled. 'Look, I'm sure you could manage, but I'd feel happier staying. It's either this or I carry you back to the hotel.'

'Okay, okay, you can stay.' She held her hands up, her cheeks flushing scarlet as her mind wandered down that particular path.

'Thank you.'

She clenched her teeth, hating how ungrateful she sounded. Here he was, coming to her rescue, and all she could do was complain. But it would be so much easier to keep on disliking him if he would just abandon her!

'So…' She tried to sound nonchalant, as if there was nothing odd about them sitting side by side on a pavement… 'You've been out for a cycle?'

'Yes.' He stretched his legs out and leaned back on his elbows. 'I ride every morning when I'm here. There are some great trails. Do you cycle?'

'Only in a gym, although I haven't done that for a while either.' She heaved a sigh. 'Obviously, I'm in worse shape than I realised. I probably got cramp because I tried to do too much again too soon.'

'That could do it.'

'*Or* this is all my sister's fault. She rang me while I was running so I stopped for a few minutes. Maybe I cooled down too much.' She stretched her leg out tentatively. 'It's kind of ironic when she's a physiotherapist.'

'Really?' He sounded interested.

'Yes, a good one too. She did a degree in sports science.' She frowned, aware that she was dropping her professional persona by revealing personal information, but needing to say something, if only to assuage her embarrassment… and to provide a distraction. She was far too aware of him sitting beside her, radiating body heat, close enough that if she leaned sideways she could have used his shoulder as a pillow if she'd wanted to.

And she was absolutely *not* going to think

about whether or not she wanted to. Just the idea was doing strange things to her insides. Her toes actually seemed to be curling.

'She's hoping to start her own business as a personal coach eventually,' she added.

'Oh, yeah? You know, all the drivers have personal performance coaches. Mine's on holiday right now, but I could ask him to share some tips, if she's interested?'

'That would be great.' She gave a tight smile. 'Aren't they worried you'll get out of shape without them?'

'Don't worry, I have a detailed list of daily exercises. Plus all the cycling.'

She gave him a sidelong look. 'You know, I never appreciated how fit drivers have to be. I mean, in a car, it looks like you're just sitting down.'

'Yeah…' His lips twitched. 'There's definitely a bit more to it than that. The hard part is staying fit without putting on too much muscle mass, and keeping a strong neck to withstand the high G-forces. Otherwise, when you go round a corner, your head feels ten times its usual weight.'

'How do you strengthen your neck?'

'I'll show you some time, if you like?' He smiled before glancing at her leg. 'How do you feel now?'

'Better, I think.' She braced her hands on the pavement to push herself up.

'Be careful.' He rose with her, wrapping a hand around her elbow as she staggered back to her feet. 'How's that?'

'Good.' She clenched her jaw. 'Pretty much back to normal.'

'Nice try. Look, just stand there for a moment, okay? Don't move.' He removed his hand slowly, as if he was afraid she might topple over without his support, then went to fetch his bike. 'Now, take my arm and we'll walk back together.'

'I really don't need—'

'Yes, you do.'

She narrowed her eyes. 'What if I use the book to tell everyone how bossy you are?'

'I don't care.'

'Fine,' she relented, curling her fingers around his forearm. It felt like a solid band of muscle.

Great... She took a deep breath, trying to ignore the silky feel of his skin as their bare shoulders bumped together. Now she was practically glued to his side. So much for keeping all her attention on the book.

'You know...' He glanced at her as they started walking, him wheeling his bike alongside. 'I could come and work at the hotel today if it helps?'

'No.' She shook her head quickly, needing to reassert some control, though it was an effort to speak when her head seemed to be pulling her in one direction and her body in the other. 'It was just a cramp, nothing an ice pack won't fix.'

'Are you sure?'

'Positive.' She nodded, shifting her posture to put a little more distance between them. She was barely breathing as it was. 'Give me twenty minutes and I'll be totally fine.'

CHAPTER EIGHT

'PULL AS HARD as you can.' Dario sat on a low chair by the window, holding a set of leather straps out to Livi. They were attached to his neck harness, a padded band that wrapped around and over his head, with small weights attached underneath.

'I don't know…' She sounded reluctant. 'Are you sure I can't hurt you?'

'Trust me, this is actually helpful. It simulates the G-forces involved in cornering and braking. If I didn't strengthen my neck muscles, I'd never be able to keep my head stable during races and then I could injure myself. Now, give it your best shot.'

'All right, but this feels weird.' She dug her feet into the floor and heaved backwards.

'Not bad. Keep going.'

'You're not moving!' She yanked harder.

'That's the whole point.'

'You could at least pretend I'm having some effect.'

'You are.'

'Liar.' She gave a short, seemingly reluctant laugh. 'How long should I keep pulling?'

'As long as you like.' He grinned as she eventually gave up. 'Want to give it try?'

She looked tempted, briefly, before shaking her head. 'No. We should get back to work.'

'Okay.' He took the harness off reluctantly. 'You're the boss.'

The problem with somebody asking endless questions about you, he thought, resuming his usual spot on the sofa, was that it made you want to ask a few of your own about them. It had been five days now since Livi had started coming to his apartment, covering everything from his earliest childhood memories to his feelings about the current set of racing regulations, and aside from what she'd inadvertently let slip about her sister the other morning, when he'd foolishly thought she'd finally been softening in her manner towards him, he didn't know anything about her.

Where did she live? Where had she grown up? What was the rest of her family like? Was she in a relationship? *Why* was she such an ice queen? He shouldn't care, he certainly didn't want to, but somehow, he couldn't seem to help himself.

It was getting harder and harder to focus on his own life when all he could think about was hers, yet every time he tried to turn the conversation around, she shut him down. As much as he admired her focus, his curiosity wasn't just piqued, it was ravenous, and the more standoffish her manner, the more intrigued he became.

He draped one arm along the back of the sofa as he watched her writing now, her pen moving across her notepad so fast it was almost a blur. He couldn't help remembering how those long, slender fingers had felt against his bare forearm when they'd walked back to her hotel. As sympathetic as he'd been about her cramp, the sight of her in figure-hugging pink and purple Lycra, so unlike her usual professional clothes, had been one of the highlights of his week.

Each time they met, he seemed to notice something new about her—the way she always crossed her left ankle over her right, her habit of sucking her bottom lip into her mouth when she was thinking, the dimple at the corner of her mouth when she *very* occasionally smiled at him. It seemed impossible now to believe that he'd ever thought of her as just another attractive woman. She was much more than that, and the extent of his interest was becoming alarming. He found himself thinking about her even when she wasn't in his apartment, so much that he'd actually looked up her social media accounts one evening, only to find them all, unsurprisingly, set to private. At this point, he would have been happy just knowing her favourite colour. All of which was bad. Very bad. He hadn't been this interested in any woman since Karolina and look how that had ended. The sooner these ten days were over and he could focus on driving again, the better. In the meantime, however…

'Why don't you type?' he asked abruptly, dragging his gaze away from her fingers before he could start wondering how they might feel elsewhere on his body.

She glanced up, a small furrow between her brows. 'I'm sorry?'

'It's just that you always bring a laptop but you never use it.'

'Oh. That's just in case I need to look something up. When I'm interviewing, I remember details better if I write them by hand. I read a study about it once. Apparently, it has something to do with brain connectivity patterns, but don't worry, I type my notes up every evening.'

'*That's* how you're spending your evenings?'

'Of course.' She seemed unperturbed by his appalled expression. 'I'm here to work.'

'You should still have some fun. It would be a shame not to see the area properly while you're here.'

She blinked, as if the idea had never occurred to her. 'Maybe when I have a revised draft.'

'You're only here for five more days.' He clicked his fingers. 'Wait. I have a great idea. Why don't you come to my race engineer's wedding in Genoa with me tomorrow? It's a beautiful drive and you could be my plus-one.'

'What?' She looked startled.

'Come to Genoa,' he repeated, feeling somewhat surprised by the offer himself. What the hell was he doing, suggesting they spend *more* time together? Had he forgotten their awkward dinner already? It was a terrible idea, not to mention wildly inappropriate. What would people think if he brought a plus-one? What must *she* think about him inviting her? The whole thing was basically asking for trouble. The wedding would be a private event, but there were always people willing to sell photos to the media. He cleared his throat, trying to think of a way to backtrack, although, fortunately, she was already shaking her head.

'Thanks, but I was going to use tomorrow to go over everything we've covered so far, just in case there are any gaps.'

'I doubt it. You've been pretty thorough.'

'Not entirely. There's still one area we haven't discussed.' She paused meaningfully. 'What happened two years ago. Not with your marriage, but your driving. I'd like to talk about that now.'

He tensed, feeling all of his muscles go rigid. Something told him she wasn't offering him a choice. 'I had a bad year, that's all.'

'You had a bad second half of the year,' she amended. 'Until then, everyone thought you were a shoo-in for the Championship. I don't mean to be insensitive, but it's hard not to think the collapse of your marriage directly contributed to your performance issues.'

He shifted in his seat. 'Like I said before, focus is important.'

'How did you feel when things started to go wrong?' She tipped her head to one side when he didn't answer. 'Readers will want to know. It'll seem strange if the book doesn't address that period at all.'

'Fine.' He flexed his fingers, stretching them out before relaxing them again. 'It felt really bad, like I'd let myself, my team and my whole family down, like everyone was calling me a failure and saying it served me right.'

'Is that what you thought?' She held onto his gaze, as if she were trying to see inside his head. 'That it served you right?'

'I thought a lot of things.'

'Okay,' she said, after letting the words hang between them for a few moments. 'Let's talk about your attitude towards the press. Before that, you always gave the impression of being happy to be interviewed. Then your whole manner seemed to change.'

'You mean when they started prefacing every question with a comment about my personal life?'

'Surely you can understand that they were only doing their jobs, reporting the facts?'

'*Facts.*' He bit the word out.

'Yes.' She quirked an eyebrow. 'Weren't they?'

He clenched his jaw as the air around them seemed to thicken and go taut. This was the exact conversation he hadn't wanted to have. And there was no way he was answering that last question…

'All right.' He thought he heard a soft sigh. 'I'll phrase it another way. It seems like your relationship with the press has never really recovered. I've been watching some of your recent interviews and you still seem to feel a lot of hostility towards them.'

'Maybe I do.' He looked towards the balcony, craving fresh air suddenly. 'Did you count the number of times I was asked about my mental state?'

'There were a lot of questions about it two years ago, I admit, but now I'd say you get the same amount as most of the other drivers. As far as I've noticed, nobody's even mentioned your divorce this year either. Do you think maybe you're a little defensive, seeing accusations that aren't really there? Have you had any counselling?'

'Yes, in the past. Now I have a therapist I talk to about driving. I don't need one for anything else.'

'But—'

'Excuse me.' He sprang off the sofa at the sound of a knock, not even pretending to look sorry as he headed for the door. Whoever it was, they had perfect timing, though it was probably just his doorman with a parcel, or Javier inviting him to play tennis again, or—

'Karolina?' He did a double take at the sight of his ex-wife, dressed in a cream-coloured maternity jumpsuit and caramel maxi cardigan, holding a bouquet of pink and white flowers. 'What are you doing here?'

'What kind of greeting is that?' she answered in English, tossing her waist-length dark hair with an expression of mock outrage.

'Sorry, it's just a surprise.' He glanced down at her bump. 'I thought you were supposed to be resting?'

'I'm still allowed to go for walks. I've just

been to the market.' She held the flowers up. 'Don't these smell gorgeous?'

He sniffed obediently. 'Sure.'

'Oh, stop looking at me like that. There's a limit to the amount of time I can spend lying around, and Jean-Michel knows where I am.' She rolled her eyes. 'Anyway, I thought I'd pop by and see if you'd changed your mind about Juliette's fashion show tomorrow evening.'

'No, I told you; I'm going to a wedding. I doubt I'll be back in time.' He lowered his voice. 'I can't really talk now either. I'm working with my biographer.'

'Right—I completely forgot about that! Pregnancy brain.' She tapped her forehead. 'I'm forgetting everything at the moment.'

'Well, you look great.' He threw a quick, cautious glance over his shoulder. The last thing he wanted was for Livi to see him and Karolina together and then start wondering about their relationship, but he could hardly shoo his pregnant ex-wife away either. 'How are you feeling?'

'Pretty good, considering that somebody's using my bladder as a trampoline. Here.' She reached for his hand and placed it over her stomach. 'Feel that?'

'Wow.' He smiled as a miniature hand or foot pushed against him. 'Does it hurt?'

'No. I love it. I feel like they're trying to communicate with me.'

'Do you need to sit down for a bit or—'

He stopped mid-sentence at the sound of a gasp, turning round to find Livi standing in the doorway to the kitchen behind him, her lips parted so wide it looked as if her jaw had just detached itself.

'I'm so sorry.' She snapped her mouth shut as their eyes met. 'I didn't mean to interrupt. I was just going to the bathroom.'

'It's fine,' Dario lied, stifling a grimace. 'Livi Thorne, meet Karolina Bonnet.'

'*Bonjour!* Welcome to Monaco.' Karolina stepped forward to kiss both her cheeks. 'I'm so pleased to meet you. If there's anything I can do to help with the book, just let me know. I'd be more than happy to fill you in on all of Dario's weird habits.'

'Karolina.' He coughed. 'I told you, we're leaving our marriage out of it.'

'Oh, right. I forgot that too.' She laughed and pretended to draw a zip across her mouth. 'My mistake.'

'And I don't have any weird habits.'

'In *your* opinion.'

'I guess I'll just...' Livi waved a hand awkwardly in the direction of the bathroom, her eyes darting between them. 'It was nice to meet you.'

'Wait. Have these.' Karolina thrust the flowers at her.

'Ohhh.' Livi looked startled again. 'I really couldn't.'

'Of course you can. In fact, I won't accept no for an answer. Here, Dario can put them in the kitchen for you for later.' Karolina beamed as she swung back towards him. 'Now, I should leave the two of you to it. Have fun in Genoa, Dario.'

'Thanks. Take care.' He stood in the middle of the hallway, a bouquet of flowers in his arms as the two women walked off in different directions. Damn it. There was no way Livi was not going to have questions about *that*.

CHAPTER NINE

LIVI STEPPED OUT OF Dario's apartment building and turned in the direction of her hotel. She hadn't intended to wrap up their interview so early today, especially since he was going to be away tomorrow. She'd had at least another hour's worth of questions planned, but seeing him with his ex-wife had thrown her. Judging by his clenched jaw when she'd returned from the bathroom, it wasn't a subject he was prepared to discuss either.

Karolina Bonnet—her new married name, according to the internet—had been the very embodiment of a pregnant glow, radiating good health and vitality, with long, sable-coloured hair, ocean blue eyes and skin so silky smooth and unblemished it must have never seen a speck of dirt, let alone a spot, in its whole life. All of that wasn't what had thrown Livi, however. *That* had been Dario's hand on Karolina's baby bump.

In all fairness, there hadn't been anything inappropriate about it. The way he'd been touching his ex-wife had been respectful rather than proprietorial, but it made no sense. It suggested that they were friends. *Good* friends, since Karolina clearly had free access to his building; there hadn't been any call from his doorman asking if she could come up. How was that possible? After the way that Dario had behaved as a husband, what kind of ex-wife would stay friends with him? How could she let him touch her at all?

Yet even more shocking had been the way Livi herself had felt at the sight of them together. It was a feeling that had started as a strange, involuntary twitch and rapidly developed into a full-blown pang of jealousy—an emotional response that was both inappropriate and completely insane. How could she be jealous? Yes, she found him attractive, and okay, maybe she didn't despise him quite as much as she had since he'd come to her rescue the other morning, but she still had *zero* romantic interest in Dario Xydis, therefore no right or reason to feel jealous. And yet the feeling was still there, lurking at the back of her mind, making her feel more uncomfortable and agitated and confused than ever.

'Livi?'

She glanced up at the sound of her name to find the ex-wife in question pushing herself up from a bench in front of her.

'Hi.' She shifted the flowers into the crook of one arm and hurried forward to offer a hand. 'Are you all right? Can I help?'

'*Merci.*' Karolina smiled gratefully. 'Standing up isn't so easy any more.'

'I'm not surprised.' Livi released her once she was safely back on her feet. 'How far along are you?'

'Seven months. Just two more to go.' Karolina smoothed her hands over her bump. 'Is your hotel this way? Would you mind if I walk with you? I'm not very fast, but it'll give us a chance to get to know each other.'

'Oh...' Livi tilted her head in surprise. Something about Karolina's expression struck her as a little too innocent, suggesting this wasn't the chance meeting she'd initially assumed. In fact, she got the distinct impression that Dario's ex-wife had been here for a while, waiting for her. Well, this was interesting... 'Sure. That would be nice. It's only a few minutes' walk.'

'Perfect.' Karolina fell into step beside her. 'So, are you enjoying your stay in Monaco?'

'Very much. Everything is so incredibly clean here, and I could definitely get used to the sunshine.' She glanced sideways, unable to resist a little digging. 'You know, I had no idea you still lived here.'

'After my divorce from Dario, you mean?' Karolina waved a hand. 'Actually, he's the newbie, not me. I'm a native Monégasque. My father was a hotel chef and my mother a maid.' She smiled. 'A lot of people think everyone here is a member of the ultra-rich elite, but there are plenty of normal residents too.'

'You're right, I'm sorry. I shouldn't have assumed.' Livi threw her an apologetic look. That was the kind of detail she ought to have known, but Dario had been so adamant about not discussing his marriage, she hadn't done much research on his ex-wife.

'It's all right. My new husband, Jean-Michel, is a native too. We actually went to school together.' Karolina's footsteps slowed a little. 'I know what you're thinking, that it must be a little claustrophobic having my ex and my new husband living so close together, but it really isn't like that. We're good friends.'

'That's…' Livi paused, trying to think of the right word '…nice? I mean, no offence, but given all the stories surrounding your divorce, it seems pretty implausible too.'

'You shouldn't believe everything you read, although I admit, our relationship was pretty bad for a while. We didn't speak for six months after our split, but then…well, maybe it helped that Monaco is a small place. It wasn't practical not to be friends.' Karolina's tone shifted again. 'So, how is the book going?'

'Pretty well, I think. The deadline is tight, but we're making good progress. I'm confident it will be finished in time.'

'Wonderful! I'm so pleased. I told Dario you'd be perfect.'

'What?' Livi swung her head round so fast, she almost lost her balance. '*You're* the one who recommended me? *You* said I was fair and impartial?'

'Yes.' The other woman nodded serenely. 'I've read all of your books. I love biographies and yours are some of my favourites.'

'Thank you. I mean, really, I appreciate that.' Livi smiled before lifting an eyebrow. 'Although I have to be honest, I think a sports journalist might have made a little more sense for this project.'

'For some parts of it, maybe, but I like your style. You don't take cheap shots at people, and you don't try to pigeonhole them. You try to really understand who they are.' Karolina's expression turned serious. 'Dario's taken a lot of abuse over the last couple of years. There have been so many negative and cruel things written about him, I thought he needed somebody fair-minded to counterbalance all that.'

'Oh…' Livi felt a twist of guilt at the words. Fair-minded wasn't exactly how she would have described her attitude towards Dario. *Man she despised... Notorious love rat... Cheating scumbag...* She cleared her throat. 'But can I ask, why does it matter to you? I mean, he's your *ex*-husband. Why do you care so much about his reputation?'

'Because he's a good person and, no matter what you've read, he wasn't a bad husband. We wanted different things from life, that's all.' Karolina rested a hand on her bump. 'This is all I've ever really wanted. Jean-Michel and I tried for a baby for fifteen months before we conceived so I'm trying to relish each day, even though I can't wait to meet this little one.'

'Well, congratulations, I'm really happy for you.' Livi stopped under the marquee of her hotel. 'This is where I'm staying.'

Karolina gave a start, clutching hold of her arm so abruptly Livi thought she must be going into labour. 'I've just had a brilliant idea! I'm going to a charity fashion show at a friend's house tomorrow evening. You should come.'

'Oh, I don't know.' She shook her head. 'Fashion shows aren't really my thing.'

'Have you ever been to one?'

'No.'

'Then how do you know?'

'Good point, but I also don't have anything appropriate to wear.'

'I'll lend you something.' Karolina looked her up and down. 'I'm a fashion merchandiser; didn't Dario tell you? I'll find you something fabulous, I promise, and don't worry about not knowing anyone. I'll look after you.' She wriggled her shoulders excitedly. 'Come on, it'll be fun. Dario's already turned me down. *Please.* I'll tell you a few stories about him, off the record, of course…' She gave a mischievous wink.

'Well…' Livi wavered. She had to admit, a fashion show did sound like fun, especially if Dario wasn't going to be there to confuse her, and it wasn't as if she had any evening plans besides working on the book. Surely she was allowed one evening off? And Karolina was being so friendly. And as for those stories… Suddenly she *really* wanted to hear them. 'Why not? That would be great, thank you.'

'Perfect. It's not an official collection, just a bunch of rich people auctioning off some old clothes for charity, but don't put your hand up and you'll be fine.' Karolina kissed her cheeks again. 'Now, I have to run, I have a pregnancy yoga class in ten minutes, but I'll get Dario to forward your number and I'll send you the details later, okay?'

'Oh…um…okay. See you tomorrow!' Livi stood where she was, watching until Karolina had rounded the corner of the hotel before pushing her way through its huge revolving doors, her head spinning.

He's a good person...wasn't a bad husband... We're good friends...

The more she thought about it, the more inexplicable the whole situation became. Not just that Karolina had recommended her, but that she'd clearly been lying in wait, wanting to talk in secret without Dario knowing. And yet everything she'd said about him had been positive. Livi racked her brains… Why wouldn't Dario want his ex-wife to tell her what a great husband he'd been? Why was he so determined not to talk about his marriage when there was clearly no acrimony between them? Why was he still so sensitive about the subject? He'd mentioned something back in London about protecting Karolina's privacy, but it seemed like more than that, as if he were protecting her personally.

She stopped halfway across the lobby, staring at the elegant wrought iron staircase that led to the bar on the mezzanine level.

Of course! She'd been making a jigsaw, but

she'd been doing it wrong, trying to force pieces into spaces where they didn't belong. But if she moved them around, tried them in different spaces… The picture coalesced and became clear in her head.

She closed her eyes to take it all in. She couldn't believe she hadn't guessed the truth sooner! If she hadn't been so blinded by her own recent experiences and prejudices, she would have.

'Miss Thorne?' A concierge approached her. 'May I be of assistance?'

'No, thank you.' She opened her eyes again, realising how strange she must look. 'I'm just realising something.'

'Ah.' He sounded as if he didn't know how to respond to that. 'Well, if you change your mind, I'll be over here.'

She sucked in a deep breath, taking another few seconds to gather her thoughts before swinging on her heel and storming back through the hotel doors, swiftly retracing her steps back to Dario's apartment building.

'Please could you tell Mr Xydis that Miss Thorne needs to see him again?' She spoke hurriedly to his doorman.

'No need.' The man inclined his head. 'He says you're allowed up any time, but I'll let him know you're on your way.'

'Thank you.' She started away and then stopped, dropping the bunch of flowers she was still carrying onto his desk. 'Would you mind looking after these for me, please?'

'Of course.'

She nodded gratefully and then headed towards the lift, her pulse thrumming as the doors closed behind her.

So much for telling her the absolute truth. She rolled the sleeves of her blazer up to her elbows as a wave of anger swept through her. Dario Xydis had a *lot* of explaining to do.

CHAPTER TEN

'HAVE YOU CHANGED your mind about coming to Genoa?' Dario was waiting in the open doorway to his apartment when Livi emerged from the lift, his dark hair tousled as if he'd needed to recover from their interview by taking a nap. 'Or did you forget something?'

'More like I missed something!' She marched along the corridor, only coming to a stop when she was standing right in front of him, curling her hands into fists and resting them on her hips. 'You know, lying to your biographer is pretty serious.'

'Lying?' He sounded bemused.

'Yes! About your divorce.' She thrust her chin up to look him straight in the eye. 'You're not the one who cheated, are you? Karolina is.'

A look of surprise flashed over his face, though it was gone almost as quickly, replaced by a half-smile that didn't reach his eyes. 'I've no idea what you're talking about.'

She gave a sceptical snort. Now they were standing face to face, she was struggling to reconcile her conflicting ideas about his behaviour. She seemed to feel relieved, baffled and enraged all at the same time. On the one hand, he wasn't a cheater, on the other, he was a liar instead. Either way, he was just like Matthew! *And* he was putting her professional reputation at stake! Just when she'd been softening towards him, too!

'That's funny, because I bumped into Karolina outside and we had a *very* interesting conversation.'

This time he couldn't hide his shock. 'She wouldn't have said anything like that.'

'You're right, she didn't. It was everything else she said that gave her away. What I want to know is why you would lie about something so huge.'

'Livi…'

'And don't you *dare* insult my intelligence again by denying it!' She leaned forward, deliberately invading his personal space. 'Tell me the truth or I'm going home and you can find yourself another biographer!'

He didn't answer, although he didn't look away either. Instead, his eyes darkened until they seemed to be made almost entirely of pupil, staring into hers with an intensity that made her breath catch and her mouth turn dry. They were standing so close she could have felt his breath on her cheek, she realised—if he hadn't been holding it, that was. Just as she was now holding hers, as if the air between them was thinner than usual, vibrating with tension. Suddenly her position felt a lot less confrontational and a lot more intimate.

A quiver of unwonted heat rippled through her body, lifting the hairs on the back of her neck and transforming her rage into something else entirely.

'So?' She took a hasty step backwards. It wasn't easy when her legs felt unnervingly like jelly.

One of his hands twitched, as if he wanted to pull her back again, before he exhaled heavily, then threw a quick look up and down the corridor. 'You'd better come inside.'

She gave a shaky nod, as if nothing awkward had just happened, stepping past him while he closed the door, then following him through to the kitchen.

'This is off the record, okay?' He went to stand on the opposite side of the breakfast bar.

'Fine.' She folded her arms, making an additional barrier between them. 'If that's what you want.'

'It is. None of what I'm about to tell you is

to go in the book, and if you share it anywhere else I'll deny everything.'

'You've made your point.' She narrowed her eyes, offended by the implication. 'I've already agreed it's off the record. So, is it true? Was Karolina the one who had an affair?'

'Yes.' A muscle jumped in his jaw. 'But I never lied to you. I never said I was the one who cheated.'

'But you knew it was what I thought!' She scowled at him. 'I told you how important honesty is to me, and you told me to use whatever information was in the public domain. You encouraged me to believe lies!'

'But I didn't ask you to spread them. Would you have preferred me to tell you the truth and then told you not to write it? As far as the rest of the world is concerned I'm the one who cheated, and that's the way it should stay. We agreed to keep my marriage out of the book, so what difference does this make really?'

'It's the principle. You promised to be completely honest with me!'

'You're right. I'm sorry.' His stern expression softened slightly. 'It's just not something I like to talk about.'

'Well, that's understandable, but it's not much of an excuse.'

'I know.' He dipped his head as he braced his

hands on the breakfast bar. 'Out of interest, how did you figure it out?'

She gave him one last accusatory look before putting her satchel down and slipping onto one of the black leather stools. 'People who've been cheated on don't wait outside their ex's building because they're determined to tell their biographer how great they are.'

'Ah.' He shook his head. 'Karolina...'

'Plus, she told me that she and her husband have been trying for a baby for fifteen months, and since she's almost full-term that means they must have started trying just under two years ago.' She lifted her shoulders. 'Either they met and got serious incredibly quickly or they were already a couple. Once I did the maths, it was pretty obvious.'

He made a rueful face. 'Nobody else figured it out.'

'You're a pretty convincing actor.' She tipped her head to one side. 'What I don't understand is why you would take the blame for something you didn't do. I mean, you must have known how it would affect your reputation. The press were brutal. Why let people think the worst of you?'

His eyes flashed. 'It's not like I wanted them to, but the truth is complicated, and honestly, all the rumours got a little out of hand. That's why I wanted to leave my marriage out of the book entirely.'

'But...'

'People will expect to read about it,' he finished for her, pushing his hands through his hair. 'I wish they'd all mind their own business.'

'Yeah...' She made a sympathetic face. 'Unfortunately, telling people to mind their own business and writing a biography don't really go together.'

He gave a short laugh. 'I guess not.'

'However, as mad as I still am at you, I guess I also owe you an apology.' She sighed. 'I know I haven't exactly been pleasant to work with.'

'You? Really?'

'Ha-ha. I'm trying to apologise, and not just for being so rude, but for believing everything I read about you. I should have known better than to be so judgemental. I *did* know better. It was hypercritical and unprofessional of me, but...'

'But?' He quirked an eyebrow when she stopped talking.

'But...' She gritted her teeth. 'It's possible that I transferred some of my feelings about my ex onto you.'

His expression shifted to one of understanding. 'Your ex cheated on you?'

'Yes.' She nodded jerkily. 'He told me about a month before our wedding.'

A strange, indefinable expression passed over his face. 'You were engaged?'

'Remember Barcelona? That was supposed to be my wedding day.'

'You mean…?' He rubbed his knuckles over his jaw. 'Damn. No wonder you looked so upset when I invited you.'

'It was pretty bad timing.'

'And then I kept you waiting for three hours after the race.'

'You did.' She rolled her eyes. 'Although it was still better than moping around at home. A change of scene was probably just what I needed.'

'I'm glad it helped.' He looked thoughtfully at her. 'So that's why you hated me on sight? That day, in your agent's office, I mean. It was because you thought I was like him?'

'In my defence, that wasn't entirely my fault. If I'd had time to prepare I could probably have pretended to be nice, but Camille sprang the whole thing on me, and the fact that you were such a notorious…' she paused to correct herself '…*alleged* love cheat struck a nerve.'

'I'm not surprised when you were going through something like that. To be honest, I'm amazed you agreed to write the book at all.'

'About that…' She scrunched her face up.

'The thing is, I kind of had an ulterior motive. Have you heard of Erin Cole?'

'The Irish singer?'

'Yes. I've loved her music since I was ten years old and it turns out she's thinking of writing a biography, which would basically be my dream project. Camille thought your book would help to raise my profile.'

'Ah. So you were using me to get to her?'

'That makes it sound more underhand than it was!' she objected. 'It wasn't like *I* deceived you. I told you I had no interest in cars.'

'True enough, I guess. In other words, you wouldn't be here if it wasn't for her?'

'Probably not. Erin just means so much to me.'

'Why?'

She was quiet for a moment, considering. 'Honestly, at first, I just liked her music. Then, as I got older, it felt like she understood me, too. I was an overachiever at school. I used to get so stressed about my grades, but somehow when I listened to her, it calmed me down. I know some people think her music is repetitive and sentimental, but she's been the soundtrack to all the big events in my life. Now it's like a comfort blanket, which is something I've needed more than ever recently.' She lifted her shoulders. 'Maybe I have been using you in a way, but my sister said to think of you as a stepping stone.' She reached into her satchel, pulling out the pebble Chloe had given her. 'She even gave me this as a reminder.'

'May I?'

'Of course.' She watched his face as she dropped the pebble into his hand. 'I was still going to do a good job for you, only… I definitely could have been nicer about it.'

'At least it makes sense now.' He turned the pebble over, smoothing it between his fingers. 'As for the book, don't worry about it. I'm happy to be your stepping stone. And for the record, I've never cheated on anybody.'

'Well, okay then.' She tried not to feel too pleased at the words. 'The question is, what do we do now?'

He looked confused. 'Can't we carry on as we were?'

'I don't know.' She knitted her brows. 'You might not have lied directly, but you withheld the whole truth. Our professional relationship relies on trust and that's broken. How can I be sure you're not hiding something else?'

'I can see why you'd think that, but I'm not, I promise.' He put the pebble back down between them.

'And I can't repeat any of those media stories

about you in the book. I'd be knowingly perpetuating lies.'

'Isn't that my choice?'

'No. It's *ours*. My name will be on the cover too.'

'Fair enough.' He looked sombre. 'In that case, whether we carry on or not is up to you. You can still walk away and we'll simply tell everyone we had creative differences. You won't lose out financially, I promise, but this is a deal-breaker for me.'

Livi glanced at the door, tension swirling in her stomach. Walking away would probably be the ethical thing to do, but on the other hand, didn't Dario deserve a decent biography, written by someone who knew the truth? Then, even if she couldn't share it, she could massage the lies a little, put them in a different kind of light, while refocusing attention on his career. Some people might say she was going easy on him, but if he won the World Championship, surely most people would want to give him the benefit of the doubt?

'No. I made a commitment and I'll stick to it.' She turned back around, surprised to see a look of relief on his face. 'I'll find a way not to repeat lies without telling the whole truth either, but only on *one* condition.' She held up her index finger. 'You have to explain to me why you took the blame.'

'Because I had to. There was no choice.' He twisted his face away for a moment. 'Okay, here's the deal. I'll tell you about my breakup if you tell me about yours.'

'What?' She jerked away from the counter. 'Why would you want to know about that?'

'Maybe because misery loves company. Or maybe because it just feels weird, you knowing so much about me when I know almost nothing about you.'

'Because I'm your biographer.'

'But this isn't for the book, remember? This is just two people talking about their failed love lives.' He spread his hands out, before bracing them against the counter again. 'That's the deal. Take it or leave it.'

'I don't know...'

She hesitated, tucking a strand of loose hair behind her ear. Sharing their stories off the record came dangerously close to blurring the lines between personal and professional. If it wasn't for the book, the story of his divorce was really none of her business. But she *was* curious, and he was right, if he was going to tell her his story then it was only fair she told him hers in return...and now that he asked, she found herself wanting to talk to somebody who'd been through something similar and would understand how it felt…

And she was staring at him, she realised, just like she'd been doing for an inappropriately long time now, just as she'd stared at him when she'd first arrived. And he was staring back again too, his eyes dark and intense, like the sky at midnight, making her heart thump erratically in response.

Oh, this was definitely dangerous, like some fairytale fantasy. She'd thought he was attractive even when she'd thought he was a cheater. Now that she had nothing to hold against him, she felt even more drawn to him. Although he *had* still deceived her, she reminded herself, even if it was only by omission. That meant he was capable of deceit, so maybe the reality was, he just hadn't cheated on anyone *yet*. After all, Matthew had been faithful until he hadn't been. Perhaps Dario would turn out to be just the same.

Despite that, she couldn't seem to tear her eyes away, as if they were being held prisoner. There seemed to be nowhere to look but at each other. What would happen if she touched him? she wondered. And was it her or had the temperature in the room just risen by several degrees?

'All right, I'll tell you about Matthew,' she

answered at last, a shiver of anticipation rippling down her spine as the last of her defences crumbled away. 'But you first.'

CHAPTER ELEVEN

'DEAL.' DARIO PUSHED himself up off the counter. 'But if we're going to discuss this, I'm going to need something to drink. What do you say? Shall we drown our sorrows together?'

Livi hesitated for a moment before nodding. 'Good idea. I'm probably done working for today anyway. Do you have any white wine?'

He walked over to the fridge and pulled out a bottle. 'Pinot Grigio? It's from a vineyard I part-own in northern Italy.'

'Perfect.' She watched as he poured two glasses, then lifted hers in a toast. 'To second impressions and not believing the worst of people.'

'Second impressions,' he echoed, clinking his glass against hers. 'And if it makes you feel any better, I thought you were an ice queen.'

She spluttered on her wine. 'How is that supposed to make me feel better?'

'I like ice queens.' He shrugged. 'It's better than being a cheating husband.'

'I guess.' She gave him a look of chagrin before arching an eyebrow expectantly. 'Speaking of which...?'

He took a mouthful of wine, swilling it around his mouth for a few seconds as he gathered his thoughts. Now that he'd agreed to talk about the collapse of his marriage, it was hard to know where to start. Aside from Ethan and his family, all of whom had been sworn to secrecy, he'd never discussed it with anybody. He'd grown so accustomed to being called a love rat online and by the press, it was sometimes an adjustment to remember he wasn't.

'Karolina is a freelance fashion merchandiser. She grew up here in Monaco, but we only met four years ago, at a photo shoot in Milan. I was completely blown away by her. She was so funny and down-to-earth, but the truth is, we should never have got married.' He looked into his glass and shook his head. 'Never make a big life decision after winning a race, especially in Las Vegas.'

Livi's lips parted, her soft intake of breath barely audible.

'She used to come with me to race weekends at first, but I was always so busy, we hardly had any time together. Plus, she hated all the cameras. She was lonely and unhappy, and it was beginning to affect her career so, after a while, it made more sense for her to stay at home.' He tightened his fingers around the stem of his wine glass. 'That's how she ended up spending so much time with one of our neighbours, Jean-Michel.'

'Oh. That's…' She stopped, as if she didn't know how to finish the sentence. 'Did you know him?'

'A little. They'd known each other in school so I wasn't even suspicious. Stupidly, I thought they were just friends.' He made a rueful expression. 'But don't get me wrong, he's actually a really good guy. We go hiking together now.'

'Hiking?' She stared at him in disbelief. 'With the man who had an affair with your wife? How do you get past something like that?'

'It takes time. When I first found out I was devastated, but after a while I realised that I was as much to blame as either of them. I wasn't a very good husband.'

'That's not what she says.'

'She's being generous. My life and hers were moving in different directions and there were things we should have discussed before we got married, like how I wanted a World Championship and she wanted a baby.' He sighed regretfully. 'She might have betrayed me, but she also deserved to be with someone who wanted the same things, although it took a lot of counselling for me to accept that.'

'But the collapse of your marriage ruined your racing season! You were leading the championship until that happened. I mean, no wonder you think racing and relationships are incompatible. Don't you resent them for all the emotional upheaval?'

'What do you think?' He gave her a sharp look. 'I was a mess for the second half of that season. I resented them both, although, in Karolina's defence, she felt almost as bad about it as I did.'

'If she felt so bad, why did she let you take the blame?'

'Because I persuaded her to. I still cared about her, and she was vulnerable. Her mother had just been diagnosed with heart disease and I didn't want her dealing with that and a load of toxic comments at the same time. Besides, she never signed up for a public life; she only ever put up with it for me. So I let her be the one to petition for divorce and then I got Ethan to spread a few rumours about me messing around.' He grimaced. 'Unfortunately, people liked the rumours a little too much. Before I knew it, the media had branded me the villain of the sport.'

'So, this whole time, you've been protecting her?' Livi's gaze moved over his face. 'Are you sure that's what she wants? Because when we talked, I got the feeling she wanted me to guess the truth.'

'It wouldn't surprise me,' he conceded. 'Neither of us expected the rumours to get quite so out of hand. Only once they'd started there was no way back.'

'Then how did you end up being friends again? Karolina said it's because Monaco is a small place.'

'That might have something to do with it, but it's also because I realised I'd rather have her in my life than not. She's a kind person, a genuine one, too, and there are a lot of phonies and backstabbers out there. Ironically, we're better as friends than we were as a couple. Aside from my family, she's one of the people I trust most.'

'Wow, that's mature.' She took another mouthful of wine. 'I can't imagine ever being friends with my ex.'

'Maybe you're just not ready yet? Anyway, when I told Karolina about the book, she said I didn't need to shield her any more, but she's happy now and I'm not going to do anything to jeopardise that, especially when she has a baby on the way. She doesn't know how vicious some people can be on social media, especially towards women.'

'That's an understatement.' Livi lifted her eyes skywards. 'You know, you're a pretty good ex-husband.'

'I had to make up for our marriage. I told you, racing demands total commitment. As narcissistic as it sounds, that makes relationships a distraction.' His chest tightened. 'It's why I don't have them any more. Aside from the risk of losing focus again, it's not fair on another person. No matter how much I care about them, in the long run, I only make them unhappy.'

She was silent for a few seconds before smiling softly. 'Well, for what it's worth, I think it was pretty noble of you to protect her.'

'Even if it almost cost me a biographer?'

'There are other biographers. You could easily have found somebody else.'

'But I wanted you.' He cleared his throat, surprised by the husky note in his voice. 'Anyway, that's what happened. For your ears only.'

'Thank you for telling me.' She inclined her head. 'And don't worry. When this book is done, you won't be the villain of the sport any more, I'm going to make sure of it.'

'I'll drink to that.' He reached across to refill her wine glass. 'Now it's your turn. Tell me about the cheater.'

'Matthew?' Her voice wavered on his name. 'Do I really have to?'

'Not if it's too upsetting, but it might help?'

She heaved a sigh. 'Okay, but I need to sit somewhere more comfortable. Come on.' She got up and headed through to the living area, collapsing onto one of the sofas and patting the space beside her. 'Here, we can sit on the same one. Then it's not like I'm interviewing you for once.'

'I like that idea.' He chuckled, sitting down beside her. 'Now, enough stalling. Matthew?'

'Right.' She seemed to steel herself. 'We met on a blind date and hit it off instantly. Everyone said we were a perfect couple because we had so much in common and, smug as it sounds, I thought so too. I thought I was lucky to have found the perfect person for me so early. Only it turns out I wasn't the perfect person for him.'

'How did you find out?'

'He blurted it out one evening after dinner.' Her shoulders slumped. 'I couldn't get my head around that afterwards. I mean, why would a person sit down to dinner like nothing's wrong when they intend to break your heart afterwards? It was like he was worried I wouldn't eat otherwise. Or maybe he just hadn't planned to tell me that evening.'

She swallowed, as if she was struggling with

the memory. 'Looking back, it seems so anti-climactic. I almost wish it had been something more dramatic, like if I'd walked in on them in bed together. Then I could have screamed and thrown things, vented properly, you know, but he was so calm and *respectful* almost. It made me feel even worse, like I was being immature for feeling upset.' She clucked her tongue. 'On top of everything else, I didn't even get a good story out of it.'

'I have a story.'

'Oh, no.' She froze. 'Please don't tell me you walked in on them in bed or I'm going to feel so guilty for saying that.'

'Not exactly. It was a bath.'

'Urgh! That's…kind of gross.'

'No kidding. It's hard to argue with two naked people. There were bubbles everywhere.' He shook his head slowly. 'For the rest of my life, I will hate bubbles.'

'But…' her eyes widened '…don't they give you champagne on the podium?'

'Yes. It's my least favourite part. Almost enough to put me off winning.'

'That's awful.' She put her glass down to press a hand over her mouth, one of her legs inadvertently brushing against his as she leaned forward. 'I'm so, so sorry. I'm not laughing at you, I promise.'

'Go ahead. In retrospect, it is kind of funny.' He arched an eyebrow. 'Now you can see why I had to give her the house. I had flashbacks every time I went to the bathroom.'

She mashed her lips together, making a strange snorting sound before erupting into peals of laughter.

'You know, I never told anyone else that part,' he said when her splutters finally subsided.

'I'm honoured.' She gave him a mock bow. 'Seriously though, it must have been a horrible shock. When Matthew told me about Sienna, I had to make him repeat it at least three times before I could process what was actually happening.' She looked sober again. 'It was such a strange sensation. One minute, I had my whole life planned out. The next, everything just fell apart.'

'I remember the feeling.'

'He moved out the same evening.' She stared hard at the table beside them. 'Do you know what's ironic? A lot of reviews say my books are psychologically perceptive and yet my own fiancé fell in love with somebody else while we were engaged and I didn't even notice. How stupid must I be?'

'You're not stupid.' He nudged his knee against hers. 'People can be good at hiding things. Karolina and Jean-Michel were sneaking around for a few months before I found out.'

'Matthew had only been seeing Sienna for a couple of weeks, or so he told me anyway.' She tipped her head back. 'I just wish he'd told me earlier, when he started having doubts about us. If he'd wanted to break up it would have been bad, but I could have dealt with it. It's the cheating part, the being replaced, that really hurts.'

'I know.'

'He even said it was a physical thing with her, like I wasn't humiliated enough. So then I did the worst possible thing and looked her up on Instagram.'

'And?'

'And she's really pretty!' She pressed a hand to her forehead. 'You know, I don't think he even meant to hurt me by saying that. It was more like an excuse, like they were a force of nature and it was all outside his control, but it made me feel soooo unsexy.'

He placed a hand on her shoulder before he could stop to think whether it was a good idea. 'How long were the two of you together?'

'Seven years, engaged for two.'

'So relationships change. It doesn't mean you're not sexy as well.'

'You don't have to say that.' She gave a loud sniff.

'I know, but I mean it. You're very sexy.'

She twisted her head, eyes wide as if she were seeing him in a whole different way. 'I wasn't fishing for compliments, but…thank you.'

'You're welcome.' He squeezed her shoulder tighter. 'Don't let him undermine how you feel about yourself.'

'That's what my sister said.'

'She sounds like a smart person.'

'I'll tell her you said so. She'll be thrilled.' She blinked at him. 'It's so weird to realise we have something in common.'

'Being sexy?'

She laughed. 'I meant being cheated on.'

'Not a great thing to have in common.'

'No. Although there's also our careers. Matthew used to say I spent too much time on my work, like I was neglecting him, but it wasn't that I didn't care. I just get so engrossed in research. I love what I do.'

'Some people don't understand what that's like.'

'Maybe that means we're better off on our own. Maybe it's like you said, some people just have to choose between a career and a relationship.' Her lips curved again, bringing out her dimple. 'And now you're going to cause me a lot of extra work.'

'I am?' He frowned.

'Yes. I'm going to have to rethink everything I've written about you so far.'

'Ah. Sorry.'

'It's okay. You're really not so bad.'

'If that's the working title of the book, we may need a rethink.' He dropped his gaze to her mouth. 'You know, this might be the first real smile you've ever given me.'

'Not true. I smiled at you five minutes ago.'

'You were laughing at my aversion to bubbles. That's different.'

'Fair enough. Shall I do it again?'

'Please.'

Her smile was even wider this time, her green eyes sparkling so contagiously he found himself smiling back. Unnervingly, they seemed to be having other effects too, specifically on the lower half of his body. He felt a sudden urge to slide his arms around her, to lift her into his lap and cover her mouth with his own.

'At least I have a day off tomorrow to revise everything,' she said, still smiling, thankfully oblivious to his thoughts.

'Unless you want to change your mind about coming to Genoa with me?' he couldn't resist offering again. Despite all the reasons why it was a bad idea, the thought of a day away from her struck him as a day wasted suddenly. 'The invitation's still open.'

'You mean to a wedding?' She made a face.

'Oh, yeah.' He grimaced. 'Sorry. That was really tactless.'

'It's all right. I don't suppose you're much of a fan either.'

'Actually, I'm back to enjoying them again. I like the optimism.'

'Then I guess there's hope for me, after all.' She leaned closer. 'Hey, can I tell you a secret?'

'Sure.'

'My sister Chloe told Matthew I was here on a romantic getaway with a millionaire. When the press release for this book comes out, he's going to think it's you.' She giggled. 'For about two seconds until he thinks about it, anyway.'

'Why only two seconds?'

'Because it's so unbelievable. I mean, *obviously*, we've decided that I'm sexy now.' She gave him an arch look. 'But not *that* sexy.'

'I don't think it's so unbelievable.'

'You don't?'

'No.'

He watched as a blush spread over her cheeks, aware of his own pulse accelerating. The air was already warm, but now he felt as though he were being heated from within too, as if the whole room was filling with electricity. He had a feeling that if either of them moved, sparks might ignite all around them. Which meant that the best thing for both of them to do was keep completely still. Only apparently his body had other ideas, since it was already moving towards her. Just as hers was moving towards his, her eyelids fluttering closed…

Their lips met and he was surprised the room didn't erupt into flames around them. All his nerves seemed to fire simultaneously, sending tremors of electricity shooting along his veins and sinews to every part of his body. There was a tremulous moment when they both seemed to be waiting for the other to pull away, and then it passed and the kiss became fierce and raw and urgent, a combination of white wine and wildfire and a heavy pounding in his blood that made it seem as though actual sparks were flickering behind his eyelids, dazzling him.

He gave a low groan as he slid his hands into her hair, cradling the back of her head. Her lips were warm and soft and she tasted so good he felt greedy with desire. He wanted to keep doing this forever. He wanted to lick and suck and nuzzle every inch of her. He wanted to lay her down on the sofa and climb on top of her. Only…

A warning bell sounded in his head. Given everything she'd just told him, what was he doing? She was obviously still vulnerable after her breakup. He remembered how that had felt, the pain of having your world fall apart, the need for reassurance and comfort. It could make a person do things they might regret in the morning. As for him, he was already way too distracted by her. A relationship, even a brief fling, would complicate things, undermine his focus…

'Wait.' He broke away, dropping his hands with an effort.

'Dario?' The way her lips formed his name almost undid him. They were swollen and red, and so tempting, he had to curl his fingers into fists to stop himself from reaching for her again.

'This isn't a good idea.' Somehow, he forced the words out. 'We've both been drinking.'

'Oh.' Her face flushed again as she wriggled away, back to her side of the sofa. 'You're right. That was so inappropriate.'

'No, it's fine, but I think…'

'I can't believe I just did that.' She leapt to her feet, evading his gaze. 'I should go.'

'What? No.' He reached a hand out. 'I was only going to say…'

'But I really should.' She was already heading back to the kitchen, sweeping up her bag and flinging it over her shoulder. 'I have work to do. Have a good time in Genoa. I hope the wedding is beautiful.'

'Livi, wait—'

'I'll see you the day after tomorrow, okay?' She ran out of the door before he could reach her. 'Bye!'

He dropped back down onto the sofa. If he wasn't careful, he was going to sabotage his focus *and* his biography, too.

CHAPTER TWELVE

A SOFT, HEAD-SPLITTING TUNE filled the air.

'Urgh, shut up…' Livi stretched a hand out from under her feather-filled duvet to stab at her phone alarm. She must have forgotten to turn it off when she'd finally crawled into bed, which meant she'd had only—her brow furrowed as she did the maths—*four hours* of sleep! No wonder she felt so wretched. Her mouth tasted like dry paper, her stomach was definitely not in the mood for breakfast, and as for her head…

She pressed her face deeper into her pillow and groaned, and not just because her body seemed to have turned against her. Her memory had joined the hate train now too, playing flashbacks of the evening before, when she'd poured her heart out to Dario and then somehow ended up straddling his lap.

What must he think of her this morning? That she was some kind of needy, insecure woman who went around asking men if she was sexy before throwing herself at them? And not just any man, but Dario Xydis. As if he'd truly be interested in a woman like her! It was beyond mortifying, especially when she was supposed to have sworn off men altogether. Her one consolation was that he hadn't seemed to mind *too* much in the moment. She wasn't even sure which of them had initiated the kiss—she'd had an impression of them both moving together at the same time—but he'd definitely been the one to pull away first.

She'd practically run back to her hotel afterwards, raiding the minibar in her room to drown her embarrassment, not that it had helped, and now that she was awake again she felt even worse. She simply couldn't believe that she'd kissed him! It had been as though, the moment she'd discovered he wasn't a cheater, she hadn't been able to restrain the attraction any longer.

Because it *had* to be just attraction, didn't it? It *couldn't* be anything deeper. Aside from their meetings in London and Barcelona, she'd barely known him for a week, and it was only two months since she and Matthew had broken up. It was much, *much* too soon to develop feelings for someone else. And even if it wasn't, and she was developing some kind of emotional attachment, how could she ever trust him when he'd already shown he could be deceitful?

On top of which, how could she risk her career, the one good thing she still had going for her? Kissing Dario hadn't been wrong exactly, even if it broke her own code of professional ethics, but if word got out, it would wreck her credibility. The reputation she'd worked so hard to establish would be critically damaged and Dario's biography would be a joke. Everyone would assume she was biased. And what if Erin Cole heard about it and refused to hire her? Considering the mess her life was in right now, she needed that project more than ever!

Oh, this was bad, *very* bad, no matter how good the kiss had been, so much that, despite her embarrassment, her lips still tingled at the memory.

She pressed her hand to her mouth and squeezed her thighs together as the feeling spread. If only she could go into denial and pretend their kiss hadn't happened, that would be something, but thinking about Dario was literally her job! At least she wouldn't have to see him today while he was in Genoa, but she was still supposed to be working on her manuscript.

For the first time in her life, she was tempted to take a sick day—which wouldn't be so far from the truth, even if it was self-inflicted—just so she could clear her head and let her subconscious work out some way to fix the situation.

Maybe she could do some sightseeing too. Dario was right, she ought to see the area properly.

And there she was, thinking about him again…

She jumped as a ringtone sounded beside her. A *ringtone*? Her stomach clenched. What if it was him?

Nervously, she pulled herself up to a sitting position, taking a deep breath before reaching for her phone and then immediately dropping it onto the bed.

Matthew?

She gaped at the screen, feeling guilty until she remembered she didn't need to. She hadn't spoken to her ex-fiancé since two days after their breakup, when he'd come to collect the bulk of his belongings. Their only communication since had been a handful of texts and emails about practical matters. So why did he want to speak with her now?

To her surprise, she realised she didn't particularly want to find out. She had enough on her mind already with Dario. But what if it was important? What if he was lying injured in a pool of blood somewhere with only a landline beside him, and her phone number was the only one he could remember by heart?

Urgh, that would be *so* typical!

Slowly, she picked her phone back up and swiped the green answer button. 'Hello?'

'Livi?'

'Yes.' She lifted her chin even though he couldn't see her. 'Is something wrong?'

'No. No, it's nothing like that, I just…' His voice trailed away. It sounded odd, strained, as if he had something difficult to say.

Oh, no... She inhaled sharply as a horrifying new thought occurred to her. What if he and Sienna were getting married and he was calling to warn her before she heard about it from someone else?

'Just what?' If he was going to say it, she wished he'd get it over with.

'I just wanted to see how you were.'

See how she was? She pulled the phone away from her ear to stare at it for a few seconds. After two months of no contact, why did he care how she was now?

'I'm fine. Why?'

'Okay, the thing is, Chloe told me you were in Monaco with some new guy?'

She bit down on her bottom lip, stifling a laugh. So *that* was the reason for his call. If she hadn't been so hungover, it would have occurred to her sooner. Obviously, his sensitive male ego was feeling insecure that she'd moved on from him so fast. Either that or he was just being nosy…

'Uh-huh.' It was an effort to keep the laughter out of her voice. 'Is that a problem?'

'No! I mean, clearly, your personal life is none of my business any more, but it just doesn't sound like you. Are you sure you know what you're doing? How long have you known this person?'

'Not long.'

'So, are you sure he's a good guy?'

Livi settled back against her cushions, the pain in her head already receding. 'Perfectly. In fact, he's a great guy. The best. Generous and kind and…' she sighed as she thought about Dario '…really magnanimous, you know?'

'Oh. Well…that's good.' Matthew's tone was more clipped suddenly. 'Obviously, I have no right to ask, but I was worried. I wouldn't want you to get hurt.'

'That's sweet, but honestly, there's no need to worry. I'm having a wonderful time. Coming here was exactly what I needed.'

'Then I'm sorry for disturbing you.' He was silent for a few seconds before his tone shifted again. 'But, Livi, if you ever do need help, you can always call me. I know I messed things up between us, but I'll always care about you.'

'Thank you.' She swallowed, taken aback by

the words. 'I mean, I probably won't call you, but it's nice to know.' She paused. 'And, for what it's worth, I hope that things work out for you and Sienna.'

'I appreciate that. Take care of yourself, okay?'

'You too.'

She set her phone back down, surprised to feel a bittersweet lump in her throat. Less like heartache, more like closure, as if their shared past still meant something. It made her *almost* regret misleading him.

She lay back down, stretching her arms over her head, although she had a feeling she was too wide awake to get back to sleep now. Despite everything, however, it occurred to her that coming to Monaco had been a good idea, after all.

As for the mess she'd got herself into with Dario, she *definitely* deserved a day off for that.

'Karolina?' Livi opened the door to her suite late in the afternoon, clapping a hand to her head as she remembered the text Dario's ex-wife had sent her the night before, the one she'd read and then completely forgotten to reply to. 'I'm so sorry, I forgot about the fashion show. I've been out sightseeing.'

'Don't worry.' Karolina waved a hand as she

swept into the room, her burgundy nails the exact same shade as her tight, one-shouldered maxi dress. 'I presumed you were busy, but you can still come tonight, right?'

'Yes!' Livi nodded vigorously. 'Absolutely.'

'Wonderful. Here.' The other woman thrust out a garment bag. 'One outfit, as promised. I had to guess your size when you didn't reply, but I'm usually right. It's vintage couture.'

'Couture?' Livi almost dropped the bag in shock. 'Are you sure it's all right for me to borrow it?'

'Of course!'

'Wow.' She peered inside, trying to keep her expression neutral at the sight of a shoulderless minidress. 'It's very bright. Sort of…metallic?'

'*Oui.* In gold and green, to match your hair and eyes. Trust me, you're going to look fabulous.' Karolina put her hands on her hips. 'Do you have any gold shoes?'

'Flip-flops?'

'*Non.*' Karolina looked horrified. 'We'll have to stop and pick some up on the way, but don't worry, they'll cost practically nothing. I have a friend who owes me a favour. It's important for where we're going, trust me. Now, you go and freshen up while I lie on this couch to stop my ankles from swelling.' She threw a playful look over her shoulder. 'If that's okay with you?'

'Go ahead.' Livi laughed, hanging the dress up carefully on the wardrobe. 'I won't be long.'

'Take your time. I promise not to look at any of your notes.'

Livi hurried into the bathroom, wondering what Dario would think if he knew she was going out with his ex-wife that evening. She hadn't got around to telling him yesterday. Would he think it was weird? Or, worse, some kind of betrayal? Only it didn't feel weird or treacherous, not when both he and Karolina had told her they were friends. Besides, it sounded like fun, attending a charity fashion show for an evening, even if it meant wearing a sparkly minidress, and at least it would stop her from worrying about seeing him again tomorrow.

She took a quick shower, then studied herself in the mirror afterwards as she wrapped herself up in a towel. After a day of eating and drinking nothing but fruit, wholegrains and water, she felt a thousand times better than she had when she'd woken up. Walking in the fresh air, wandering along the Place du Casino and exploring the Oceanographic Museum had given her skin a rosy glow too. Even her hair, which she'd washed and styled that morning, had a tousled, beach wave look. Maybe she really was a little bit sexy…

She smiled at her own reflection. It was time

to glam up, let her hair down, put on some vintage couture and go out.

An hour and a half later, her feet encased in a pair of new gold leather mules, Livi found herself sitting in the passenger seat of Karolina's Maserati as they drove through the gates of a large art nouveau style villa in La Turbie, an ancient-looking village in the hills overlooking Monaco.

'What a beautiful house.' She felt as if she'd just entered the pages of some high-end architectural magazine. The driveway was lined with fig trees, while the building itself appeared to have grown straight out of the hillside, all flowing lines, wrought iron balconies and terracotta ceramic tiles, with sweeping vistas of the Mediterranean below.

'It was built in the nineteen-twenties,' Karolina told her, draping her long dark hair over one shoulder as they climbed out of the car. 'Juliette's family have owned it ever since.'

'Juliette?'

'Juliette Riqueti.'

'The shoe designer?' Livi came to a halt in the middle of the driveway. 'This is *her* house?'

'Yes.' Karolina reached for her arm, pulling her out of the way of an approaching Lamborghini Aventador. 'Her children took over the company several years ago, so she's retired now, but she and her husband still like to put on charity events.'

'So this is why you were so bothered about my footwear?'

'I didn't want you to feel conspicuous. *Bonjour*, Juliette.' Karolina stretched her arms out as they approached the door, speaking in English as she pressed kisses to the cheeks of an elegant-looking older woman, whose soft grey lob perfectly framed her round face. 'This is the friend I was telling you about, Livi Thorne. She's a writer.'

'Of course.' The woman smiled at Livi. 'I'm so pleased you could make it.'

'Thank you so much for including me.' Livi resisted the temptation to curtsey.

'Not at all. The catwalk is right by the pool. Go and make yourselves comfortable and help yourself to a cocktail—or mocktail in your case.' Juliette looked fondly at Karolina. 'You look incredible, by the way. *Vous êtes rayonnante.*'

'*Merci, et tu es trop gentil.*'

They walked into the villa, through a glass atrium that led straight onto a large terrace with a Roman-style swimming pool surrounded by immaculately landscaped gardens. Pink lanterns hung from lines running between the trees, casting a warm glow over the hundred or so people already gathered, reclining on sun loungers or sitting at tables, while a DJ played on decks set up beside the diving board.

'I don't know what I expected, but this is amazing,' Livi murmured, leaning closer. 'I feel like such an imposter.'

'Don't be silly. Juliette loves artists of all kinds.' Karolina squeezed her arm. 'By the way, did I tell you I spoke to Dario this morning?'

'No.' Livi tensed, wondering what she was about to say next.

'He told me you guessed the truth about our divorce.' Karolina lowered her voice. 'You must think I'm a terrible person.'

'Not at all.' She shook her head quickly. It was strange, considering how prejudiced she'd been towards Dario, but she didn't feel any kind of negative feeling towards Karolina. It struck her as more proof that she was getting over Matthew.

'Thank you.' Karolina sounded relieved. 'To be honest, I'm glad that you know. I don't like keeping secrets. Now we can all relax tonight and be happy.'

'*We?*' Her steps faltered.

'Yes. Dario said he might stop by on his way back from Genoa.'

'He did?' She felt a flutter of panic. 'Does he know I'll be here?'

'Of course. Oh, look, there's Jean-Michel!' Karolina waved to a handsome sandy-haired man in a beige suit standing beside the pool.

'You must be Livi.' He came over to greet them, extending a hand towards her. 'I'm glad to meet you. I've saved us a spot.'

'Just in time.' Karolina grasped his hand as he led them towards a table. 'It looks like the show is about to start.'

Livi sat down beside Karolina, carefully tugging the hem of her dress over her thighs as Juliette emerged from the villa, waved to her guests and then took a seat just as the music turned up and a row of models poured from a nearby pool-house.

She willed herself to relax as they strutted past, dressed in an eclectic range of outfits from ballgowns to business suits to swimwear, but Karolina's words had thrown her. Then again, what were the odds of Dario stopping by really? He'd probably be exhausted after the wedding, and she doubted he'd want to see her again so soon after yesterday anyway. As for how she felt about the prospect of seeing him again, she had no idea how she felt about that. She probably wouldn't know until she actually set eyes on him…

No sooner had the thought entered her head than she felt a tingling sensation on the back of her neck. Slowly, she twisted her head, her heartbeat thumping so loudly it practically drowned out the music. As she'd somehow expected—*known*—Dario was standing in the doorway to the villa, dressed in a dark blue suit and white shirt, looking straight at her.

CHAPTER THIRTEEN

DARIO CLOSED HIS EYES and then opened them again as a bolt of heat shot through him. The woman sitting on the other side of the terrace looked like the woman he'd kissed last night, only a sparklier, shinier, even more stunning version.

Livi?

He'd only half meant it when he'd told Karolina he might join them tonight. Going to Genoa had been fun, but it had been a long day and he was tired. He wasn't sure how Livi would feel about seeing him again either, especially in the company of his ex-wife. She might prefer to discuss what had happened between them in private, or not at all considering how quickly she'd fled his apartment last night, but after twenty-four hours of writing and deleting texts, trying to decide whether or not to call her, all while trying to enjoy somebody else's wedding, he hadn't been able to wait to see her any longer.

Knowing what to say on the other hand… Their kiss had been a mistake, obviously, and yet he couldn't quite bring himself to regret it either. All he knew was that he wanted to set things right between them. And now there she was, looking across the terrace towards him, an indefinable expression on her face that was probably a mirror image of his own, looking so stunning that he felt a powerful craving to go over there and haul her into his arms, to carry her off to some secluded spot and…

'Livi?' He found himself standing beside her before he even knew he was moving.

'Dario.' She gave him a wary smile. 'How was the wedding?'

'Perfect. I've never seen my engineer so happy.' He nodded to Karolina and Jean-Michel before slipping into the empty chair beside her. 'How was your day? You haven't been working too hard, I hope?'

A faintly guilty expression passed over her face as she shook her head, making her hair bounce around her shoulders in a way that made him want to reach out and stroke it. This was the first time he'd seen it loose and it was even more vibrant and lovely than he'd expected.

'Actually, I took a day off like you suggested and went sightseeing. I haven't written a single word.'

'Dario, you made it.' Karolina leaned across the table towards him. 'Doesn't Livi look gorgeous?'

He quirked an eyebrow at his ex-wife's enthusiasm. He hadn't told her about the kiss and he very much doubted Livi had either. 'She does. Extremely.'

'Karolina loaned me the dress.' Livi gestured awkwardly downwards.

'It looks good. I mean, different to your normal clothes, but good different. Not that I don't like what you usually wear.' He cleared his throat before he could trip over his tongue any more, trying to distract her by gesturing towards the catwalk. 'Have you seen anything you like?'

'In the show?' She gave him a faintly incredulous look. 'I'm not really a couture kind of girl. When I'm not working, I'm usually in jeans and T-shirts.'

'Maybe you should buy her something?' Karolina interrupted again. 'It's for charity, after all, and there was a red gown a couple of minutes ago that…'

'No!' Livi interjected quickly. 'You really don't need to buy me anything,' she said to Dario. 'I already bought some new shoes tonight.'

'I tried to pay, but she wouldn't let me.' Karolina shrugged.

Dario glanced down at Livi's feet, letting his gaze linger briefly on her bare legs before hoisting it back up again. 'They're very nice.'

Thankfully, he was prevented from making any more awkward comments about her appearance as the music quieted and Juliette went to stand at the end of the pool with a microphone.

He leaned back in his chair, only half listening as the designer launched into a speech. He was vaguely aware of the models lining up along one side of the pool too, presumably to give potential buyers one last chance to look at the outfits before bidding began, but he was far too busy studying Livi out of the corner of his eye to care.

To his relief, she didn't seem upset or angry with him. She hadn't thrown her cocktail into his face yet anyway, although, judging by the stiff set of her shoulders, he got the impression she was putting on a show of normality for Karolina and Jean-Michel. He wouldn't know how she really felt until he got her alone…

'Aren't you going to bid?'

'Mmm?' He gave a jolt, realising that Karolina was speaking to him again. He hadn't even noticed the auction starting. 'No, I don't think so.'

'Dario, it's for charity.'

'I'll give a donation.'

'Spoilsport.'

'Fine.' He turned to Livi. 'What do you think?'

Her lips twitched as she pointed towards a male model wearing a leopard-print nineteen-seventies style suit. 'What about that? Then we'll match.'

'The craftsmanship is actually amazing.' Karolina nodded enthusiastically. 'Plus, it would really suit your colouring.'

'Okay, but you bid for me. I'm too tired.' He lowered his voice to Livi. 'Now see what you've done?'

'Sorry.' She appeared to be suppressing a giggle.

'Walk with me?'

'What?' Her expression sobered instantly. 'Now?'

'Unless you want to listen to the bidding?'

'Not particularly, but isn't it rude to leave?'

'Not if I buy that suit. We won't be long,' Dario murmured to Karolina as they stood up and made their way towards a tiled path through the fig trees behind them.

'So…' Now that he had Livi alone, he wasn't sure how to begin. 'You and Karolina seem to be getting along well?'

'Yes.' She kept her gaze straight ahead. 'You're right, she's very kind.'

'I don't suppose you told…?'

'*No!*' she answered vehemently. 'I don't know why she's…' She glanced at him and winced. 'Look, this might sound odd, but do you think she's…?'

'Matchmaking?' He nodded. 'Possibly. She's always telling me I ought to start dating again. I'm sorry if it's making you uncomfortable.'

'It's not that, it's just…you know, a little weird.'

'Yeah. I'm hoping that once the baby is born she'll direct her attentions elsewhere.'

'At least that explains this dress.' She put her hands on her hips. 'This is officially my first time in anything this tiny *or* this gold.'

'A momentous night then?'

'Extremely.'

They walked on in silence for a while. The trees in this part of the garden were hung with green rather than pink lanterns, making her dress seem to glow even brighter.

'Livi, about last night—' he began as they reached a small clearing.

'I know,' she interrupted him. 'My behaviour was completely unprofessional. I can't believe I kissed you.'

'Hey.' He reached for her arm, bringing them to a halt beneath a wooden arbour, half-covered with grapevines. 'It wasn't just you. It was mutual. We were both drinking and talking about our past relationships. We kissed each other.'

'We did?' Her shoulders sagged. 'That's such a relief. I couldn't remember and then I was afraid I'd thrown myself at you.'

'And I was worried you'd think I took advantage of the situation.'

'Is that why you stopped?' A pink flush spread over her cheeks. 'It wasn't because it was…bad?'

'Bad?' He frowned. 'Not at all. Why? Is that what you thought?'

'No.' Her breath sounded a little uneven suddenly. 'As kisses go, it was…'

'Really good.'

'Yes.' She looked relieved. 'Sorry. I'm just being paranoid. Some of the things Matthew said really got into my head.'

'Livi.' He placed his hands on her shoulders. 'It was a great kiss, trust me, but there are reasons…'

'*Lots* of reasons,' she agreed. 'It was an intense situation and we got carried away, that's all.'

'Exactly.' He had to force himself not to look at her mouth again. 'So, are we okay?'

'Of course.' She nodded so emphatically her head looked in danger of falling off. 'We should just forget it happened and get back to normal.'

'That would be great. I mean, obviously there's some chemistry between us…'

'But that doesn't mean we should act on it.' She was still nodding. 'We have bigger priorities. I have a book to write and you have a championship to win. We both need to focus on our careers.'

'Absolutely.' He smiled, wondering why he didn't feel more relieved. Yes, he was glad they'd talked it through, but he was aware of a sharp pang of regret too, as if he'd just missed some important chance.

'Phew!' She heaved a sigh, leaning back against one of the wooden posts of the arbour. 'I'm so glad we agree. I mean, us being together would be a huge conflict of interests. I'm writing a book about you! I'm supposed to be impartial, not part of the story. If the press found out, they'd have a field day. It could ruin my professional reputation and damage your image even more.'

'Huh.' He paused. 'I guess. I hadn't thought about it that way.'

'Plus, in a week's time I'll be back in England and you'll be racing again.' She went on. 'Our lives are so far apart, they're practically on different planets.'

'Right. Although…' he rested a hand on the

grapevine beside her '…just for argument's sake, lives can come together.'

'Yes, but you're the one who said that driving and relationships don't mix.'

'I did,' he agreed firmly. 'And you're vulnerable. You just broke up with your fiancé.'

'Not *just*. It was over two months ago now.'

'But it must still feel raw?'

'Actually…no.' She sounded thoughtful. 'Weirdly enough, he called me this morning. How's that for timing?'

'The cheater?' He moved a step closer, effectively pinning her against the post, seized with a completely inappropriate rush of jealousy.

'Matthew, yes.' Her expression remained tranquil. 'You know my sister told him I was here? Well, he wanted to make sure I was all right. It was actually nice in a way, to know he still cares, even if it's just as a friend. It made me realise how far I've come. I didn't feel pain or regret or even anger any more, just… I don't know, nostalgia.'

'But that's good, isn't it?' *He* definitely thought so, even if he shouldn't.

'Ye-es.' She looked conflicted. 'Although part of me feels guilty that I got over him so quickly. I mean, we were supposed to be married by now. It makes me wonder whether our relationship had more problems than I wanted to admit.'

She scrunched her mouth up for a few seconds. 'I still wish he hadn't cheated, but, as much as I hate to admit it, maybe we both fell out of love a while ago, and I just didn't realise.'

'You're being too hard on yourself.' He fought the urge to reach up and smooth away the slight crease between her brows. 'It can be difficult, letting go of a relationship, especially when you loved that person once. Sometimes we don't want to see what's right in front of us.' He quirked an eyebrow. 'Would it be better if you were still crying into your pillow every night?'

'Definitely not.'

'Then you shouldn't feel guilty. You're just… recovering.'

'I am.' She peered up under her lashes at him. 'You know, I've felt much better since I came here, like I've finally moved on, so you definitely weren't taking advantage last night, no matter how needy I might have been.'

'You weren't needy. No more than I was anyway.'

'Excuse me, but you didn't whine until I told you how sexy you were.'

'That's true.' He rubbed a hand over his chin. 'Although I'm still devastated you didn't volunteer the information.'

She gave a startled laugh. 'Go online. I'm

sure there are plenty of people there who'll tell you how sexy you are.'

'Maybe I don't care about people online.'

'Then go and talk to all those screaming fans at your next race.'

'You're going to make me beg, aren't you?'

'So insecure…' Her lips curved. 'Fine. You're sexy too.'

'*Just* sexy?' He tilted his head to one side. 'Didn't I call you "very sexy"?'

'You want an adverb? Okay. You're *extremely* sexy.'

'Thank you. Was that so hard?'

'No, but if you're not careful, your ego is going to be too big to fit back in your apartment.'

'You might be right.' He patted his head, as if he were checking its size, loving the way she laughed again.

'Oh!' she exclaimed, lifting a hand abruptly. 'Listen!'

'What am I listening to?'

'That's one of Erin's songs. *Love on a Runway.* It's one of my favourites.'

He opened his mouth to ask her to dance and then closed it again. They'd literally just cleared the air. Wrapping his arms around her would be another reckless idea. It occurred to him suddenly that bringing her here, to such a secluded, romantic setting, with her in that dress, was already playing with fire.

He coughed and took a step back. 'We should get back to the party.'

'Good idea.' She still seemed distracted by the music. 'Karolina might have bought you a whole new wardrobe by now.'

'Don't even joke about that.' He rolled his eyes as they started back along the path. 'So, tell me more about your sightseeing today. Did you have fun?'

'I did, although it'll probably sound clichéd to you. First, I went to the Place du Casino and had a coffee in the Café de Paris, then I wandered around the Metropole shopping centre looking at all the designer shops, and then I walked along the waterfront to the Oceanographic Museum, which was incredible. Oh, and I almost went on a boat tour to do some snorkelling, but I ran out of time.'

'Have you been snorkelling before?'

'Just once on holiday, but I really enjoyed it.'

'Then why don't we do it tomorrow morning?' he offered impulsively.

'I don't know.' She gave him an uncertain look. 'We only have four days together left. We should really get back to work.'

'We can go early. It won't take more than

an hour, and I know a great place not far from your hotel.'

She hesitated for a moment and then smiled. 'Okay. That does sound fun.'

'Perfect. Meet me outside your hotel at seven and we'll be back in time to start work at nine. Just bring your swimsuit and a towel and I'll bring the rest.'

'I'll be there.'

'Great.'

He fell into step beside her as they carried on along the path, glad that he'd come tonight after all. Talking had been absolutely the right thing to do. Yes, they were attracted to each other, but they were also mature grown-ups who could control themselves. And now that was settled they could put the kiss behind them and simply enjoy each other's company. They had so much in common, it would be strange if they couldn't be friends. As for inviting her to go snorkelling with him, that was completely harmless. It wasn't as if they were likely to throw themselves at each other under the water.

So why did he get the feeling he was kidding himself?

CHAPTER FOURTEEN

'YOU WEREN'T EXAGGERATING about it not being far.' Livi stood beside Dario on Larvotto Beach the next morning, watching the turquoise waves lap gently against the shore. They were so close to her hotel she could almost have picked up one of the tiny pebbles beneath her feet and thrown it onto her balcony. Behind them, hotel workers were busy setting out cream-coloured sun loungers and parasols for the day, but there was only a scattering of other tourists around.

'There were other beaches we could have gone to, but this is good for beginners.' Dario flashed her a wide grin. 'Plus, I like swimming here at this time of the morning, before the crowds arrive. It's a perfect start to the day.'

'It's definitely pretty at this hour.' Livi tipped her head back and sucked in a deep breath, filling her lungs with fresh sea air as she soaked in the pale morning sunshine. She was glad now that she'd dragged herself out of bed so early, despite it being almost two a.m. by the time Karolina and Jean-Michel had dropped her back at her hotel. This time she'd slept well, however.

Thank goodness she and Dario had talked last night. It meant they could both now relax and enjoy this experience without any awkwardness. As for the way her heart had jumped when she'd seen him outside her hotel ten minutes ago…well, feelings like that could be overcome. Just like the violent thump of her pulse when he'd removed his shirt, revealing rock-hard abs and a washboard stomach, could be overcome. Because they were both being sensible, focusing on their careers. Any kind of intimacy between them would only be asking for trouble, especially when she didn't know if she could trust him. And with any luck, a quick dip in the Mediterranean would be just as effective as a cold shower…

'Wait, is that a net?' she asked, her stomach fluttering in alarm as her gaze settled on a line of small white buoys floating in the harbour. 'Is the water dangerous?'

'No, but the currents are stronger further out.' Dario's tone was reassuring. 'The net's there mainly to stop jellyfish getting close to the shore. Here—' he passed her a snorkel vest '—the water might still be a little chilly.'

'Thanks.' She put the vest down by her feet

while she pulled her powder-blue sundress over her head, revealing a white plunge bikini underneath. Despite bringing a sensible black one-piece to Monaco with her, she'd found herself impulse purchasing the bikini in the Metropole shopping centre the day before. It was a little impractical for snorkelling, but it would have been a shame *not* to wear it, even under a sleek-fitting vest.

'You'll need these too.' Dario handed her some flippers, though he seemed to be keeping his eyes averted.

'Very glamorous.' She zipped the vest up and bent over, kicking off her sandals and wriggling her feet into the flippers.

'Is the fit comfortable?' His voice sounded curiously husky now.

She lifted her feet up and down. 'Yes.'

'Okay. Now you just need your mask and snorkel and you're all set.' He darted a quick look sideways. 'I've already treated it for fogging.'

'Great.' She pulled the mask over her face, adjusting the fit until it was snug but not tight, the way she'd been taught.

'Ready?' Dario's voice was muffled behind his own mask.

She gave him a thumbs-up and then waded

out into the shallows, her chest buzzing with excitement as the waves lapped against her legs.

The water was cool like Dario had said, but not too cold, and as pristinely clean as everything else in the Principality, making the visibility perfect. She swam out a few metres to warm up and then spread her arms and legs out, floating face-down on the surface. Almost immediately, a shoal of fish appeared beneath her, a vibrant shimmer of silver and gold like a constellation of stars beneath the water. For a moment they seemed to hang there, as if they were curious about what she was doing, before losing interest and darting away, swimming off into an ethereal world of white sand and pale green water.

She kicked her feet gently to follow them, floating over patches of red coral, a few sea urchins, a couple of crabs and a few stray amber-coloured fish she couldn't identify. At one point she felt a tap on her leg and turned her head to find Dario pointing to a larger blue and silver fish on the other side of the net. She nodded at him, enveloped in a sense of deep-seated peace and contentment.

For the first time in a long time, she felt as if she could finally turn her thoughts off and exist purely in the moment. Somehow, being underwater put her own life and problems into perspective too. Just knowing that there was a whole other world down here, one that didn't care about biographies or failed weddings or racing drivers, made her feel as if none of those things really mattered. She doubted she would have felt quite so peaceful if she were out in the open sea where there were a lot more dangers, but swimming here, close to the shore, she felt completely free and protected.

'That was amazing!' she called to Dario, pulling her mask off as she staggered out of the water a little while later. 'I felt so relaxed.'

'I'm glad you enjoyed it.' His gaze swept over her briefly before settling back on her face. 'Come on. There's a shower just up the beach. We can leave our gear here while we rinse off the salt.'

'Good idea,' she agreed, dropping her flippers and vest onto the sand, then following him past a lifeguard tower towards an outdoor shower station. 'So, do you do this often?'

'Not often.' He seemed to be avoiding looking at her again. 'I prefer diving. There are some great coves around the coast. I find that being in nature helps to keep things in perspective, you know? Especially all of the glitz and glamour that goes with racing. It can be fun, but it's important to remember it's not real.'

'That's exactly what I felt down there.' She

smiled in agreement. 'That sense of being unimportant, but in a good way.'

'Here we are.' He stopped beside the shower, his chest only inches from hers as he slipped past to push the button. 'You first.'

'Thanks.' She closed her eyes as she dipped under the water, wanting to hold onto the feeling of peace a little longer. 'How do you get to these coves anyway? Don't tell me you own one of those boats in the harbour?'

'Something like that.'

'No way.' She opened her eyes again, just in time to see him wrench his gaze away from a spot just below her navel. 'You own a superyacht?'

'It's more of a big boat.' He coughed. 'A yacht requires a crew. I'd rather go out by myself or with a few friends.'

'That makes sense.' She pushed her hands through her hair, squeezing out the excess water before stepping aside. 'Your turn.'

She looked towards the sea while he showered behind her, not trusting herself not to ogle his abdominal muscles again otherwise. It was so warm already, she didn't even need a towel to dry herself off. He was right, this had been the perfect way to start the day, although she was going to need something to eat before they started work. All of that swimming had given her an appetite.

'How about I buy you breakfast as a thank you?' she offered, over her shoulder. 'Unless you're afraid of being recognised?'

'Not really.' He laughed, shaking himself off as he came to stand beside her. 'There are plenty of famous people in Monaco. I'm nothing special.' He glanced at his watch. 'But we only have half an hour until nine.'

'Half an hour?' she gasped, letting her gaze linger briefly on the muscles of his shoulders and neck. 'How long were we in the water?'

'About an hour.'

'No way! I thought it was maybe twenty minutes. I completely lost track of time.'

'Well, I'm happy to start work a little later, but it's up to you.'

She didn't answer at first, thinking as they walked back along the beach. If she was being truly sensible she'd renege on her offer and meet him at his apartment at nine as usual. She'd have just enough time to go back to her room, get dressed and grab a croissant on her way out, but what harm could a breakfast do?

'We can start late,' she agreed finally, slipping her sundress back over her damp bikini. 'My hotel has a coffee shop out front. It's usually quiet in the mornings.'

'Sounds good.' He looked pleased, shrugging his shirt over his shoulders, though he left it unfastened.

'All right then, what can I get you?' She gave him an assessing look as they gathered up their belongings and started back up the beach. 'I don't suppose you have fry-ups here?'

'Not normally, no, but an espresso and brioche would be perfect.'

'Really? Don't you have to stick to a diet of muesli and fruit?'

'It's the summer break. I'm allowed to break the rules a little.'

'In that case, why don't we do today's interview out on your balcony? I don't feel like sitting inside any more.' She threw him a half-teasing, half-remonstrative look. 'Although this is all your fault for encouraging me to get out and about.'

'Better still, why don't we walk and talk? Now you've made a start with sightseeing, I could give you a local's tour. The Marché de La Condamine is definitely worth a visit, and I know a great place for gelato. We could call it a field trip.'

'I don't know.' She felt hesitant again. 'It wouldn't be very good for recording. Plus, a market might not be the best venue for sharing personal stories.'

'You know them all already.' He darted her a smile. 'How about I promise not to say anything particularly interesting?'

'Um…'

'Or we talk about less controversial subjects. I bet you can't guess my favourite gelato flavour.'

'Strawberry?'

'How did you—' He pretended to look shocked before shaking his head. 'Not even close.'

She laughed as they stopped outside the café, turning to look back at the sea, though she could still feel his gaze on her face. Going on a walking tour with him sounded more like fun than work, but they were friends now…and she was still feeling relaxed, even if her breathing was somewhat on the shallow side…

'Livi?'

She looked back at him. His hair was tousled from the shower, sticking up a little at the back. It made her want to reach up and smooth it down. And maybe stroke the nape of his neck while she was at it… Which was exactly why she ought to say no and insist they keep things professional by limiting work to his apartment instead. It was bad enough that they were going to start late. If she kept on breaking her own rules, what would she agree to next? Only somehow, the words refused to come out.

'Why not?' She lifted a shoulder, ignoring the warning voice in her head. 'But brioche first.'

'Absolutely.' His smile was even wider than before.

'And I definitely want to visit that gelato place.'

'Not a problem.'

'Good.' She dropped the snorkelling equipment beside a table. 'You wait here. I'll get us some breakfast.'

It would be fine, she told herself as she headed towards the counter. Better than fine—*fun*. She just needed to stay strong. Strong and very, *very* focused.

'I can't decide. It's impossible!' Livi looked up and down the frozen display counter before them. There were three rows of tubs, each containing ten different flavours of gelato. 'They all look so delicious.'

'They do,' Dario agreed, trying not to laugh at the earnest look on her face.

'I mean, I want two scoops, so you'd think it would be easier, but some flavours just don't work together. I mean, mint with orange? I don't think so.'

'Then have three scoops.' He raised an eyebrow. 'You know, this is supposed to be a treat, not something to cause anxiety.'

'Ice cream is my greatest weakness.' She gave him a sombre look.

'Wow. Okay.' He resisted the urge to put a hand on the small of her back as she leaned over again. 'Do you want me to choose for you?'

'Absolutely not. What if you chose wrong? I'd resent you forever. What *is* your favourite anyway?'

'Bacio and cappuccino, *merci*.' He nodded to the server waiting patiently behind the counter.

'That actually sounds really good.'

'So…?'

'One more second.' She flexed her fingers. 'Okay, I've decided.'

'Are you certain?'

'Don't ask me that or I might change my mind again!' She turned to the server. 'I'll have one scoop of pistachio and one of stracciatella in a waffle cone, *s'il vous plaît*.'

'Excellent choice.'

Two minutes later, it occurred to him that he hadn't entirely thought through his offer of gelato. Livi was literally moaning in the street. It was hard enough not thinking about the way she'd looked in her bikini that morning—the bikini he knew she was *still* wearing beneath her dress—but watching her lick ice cream was another level. A shiver that had nothing to do with the temperature of his gelato rippled through him. He needed to end this tour soon or he'd go out of his mind.

'Oh, my goodness…' she moaned again as her tongue circled the rim of her cone. 'This is *soooo* good.'

He grunted, not trusting himself to say anything coherent.

'There must be some kind of special ingredient. Is there?' She swung round to look at him. 'I mean, is there a secret recipe or something?'

He coughed. 'I have no idea.'

'I mean, honestly, this is the best ice cream I've ever tasted.'

He finally managed to master himself. 'Just like the brioche you ate for breakfast was the best you've ever had?'

'What can I say? It's been a good day for food.'

'Between all the swimming and walking, I think we've earned it.'

'True.' She finished the last of her gelato cone, licking her lips with a happy, satiated expression. 'So, where next?'

'Next, I have to go to the gym. It may be the summer break, but I still have a training regime.'

'Fair enough. I should write up my notes from today anyway.'

'But we could go out again this evening?' he

found himself suggesting impulsively. 'There's an open-air cinema on Le Rocher. It's right next to the sea, so if you get bored with the film you can admire the view.'

'That sounds amazing,' she answered enthusiastically.

'And maybe tomorrow we could go out on my boat?' For some reason, he was still talking, making suggestions before his brain could catch up. 'It's going to be a beautiful day.'

'Oh.' Her eyes widened with a surprised look.

He tensed, feeling somewhat surprised at himself too. What was he doing? It sounded like he was setting up a series of dates! A 'friendly' walking tour was one thing, but everything else was a terrible idea. Clearly, he was still under the sway of white bikinis and watching her eat ice cream…

'Actually, maybe we should—' he started to backtrack.

'You mean, your "big boat"?' she interrupted, a faint smirk on her lips.

'Ye-es.' He felt his lips own twitch in reply.

'Well, I would like to see that. I've been looking at the boats in the harbour all week and wondering what it would be like to go out on one.' She paused. 'But we'll still be working, right?'

'Of course. What else?'

'Well, all right then.' She smiled. 'That sounds lovely.'

'Great.' He nodded, not knowing whether to be pleased or to grab his bike and flee for the hills.

CHAPTER FIFTEEN

'WHAT ARE YOU DOING?' Javier demanded, striding across the basement gym of the apartment building towards Dario. It was five a.m. and so far, they were the only two people crazy enough to be exercising at this hour.

'Kettlebell lifts.' Dario huffed a breath as he heaved the weights. 'Why?'

'You're extending too far.' Javier gestured towards his hips. 'Much as I'd like to gain some advantage over you, you'll strain your spine if you're not careful.'

'Damn. Thanks.' He set the kettlebells aside. 'I guess I wasn't paying attention.'

'No kidding. Anything wrong?'

'No. I was just…thinking.'

'Uh-huh.' Javier gave him a long look before sitting down on a bench opposite. 'This wouldn't have anything to do with a certain hot writer, would it?'

'*Hot?*' He felt a flash of jealousy at the description.

Javier arched an eyebrow. 'You don't think so?'

'That's not what I meant.' He wiped a hand across his brow and reached for his water bottle. 'I just didn't realise you'd noticed.'

'I notice a lot of things. For example, I was at the open-air cinema yesterday, and I noticed the two of you sitting together.'

'We were watching the movie.'

'Really? Because it looked like your eyes were on her most of the time. I would have come over to say hi, but I didn't want to intrude. You have it bad, my friend.'

Dario stiffened defensively. 'We're working together, that's all.'

'Then tell me what the movie was about?' Javier stood up with a grin. 'Hey, I'm not judging. You can do what you like. Now, I'm heading out for a run, but don't overdo it with the weights, okay? Save your energy for other activities.' He winked.

'There *aren't* any other activities.'

'Pity. It's about time you had some fun.'

Dario made a rude gesture, eliciting a chuckle from the other driver as he strode away. It didn't help his mood that every word Javier had just said had been true. He *had* been thinking about

Livi before, he *had* been careless with his weight training, and he had absolutely *no* idea what last night's movie had been about. Because he'd been distracted.

He stretched out on the mat to do some planks. The blunt truth was that the situation with Livi was getting out of control. He'd thought they could be friends, but he'd started enjoying her company a little too much for comfort. He'd particularly enjoyed sitting beside her in the twilight, sharing a bucket of popcorn while some kind of alien invasion had played out on the big screen, but that was just another sign he needed to nip this thing in the bud before he did something stupid.

Every time they were together, he let his guard down a little more, and he couldn't take the risk of falling for her, not when they both had so much at stake. Unfortunately, he'd already invited her out on his boat today *and* arranged a champagne picnic. If he had any sense he would cancel, but what excuse could he give?

Then again, she was leaving the day after tomorrow, something he realised he'd been trying not to think about, and then everything would get back to normal. He was probably overreacting anyway, since she clearly wasn't interested in a relationship—she'd even made a point about bringing her work today! As long as he focused on answering her questions, there wouldn't be a problem. And if she was wearing her white bikini again, he'd simply look in the other direction and think unsexy thoughts about jellyfish.

Because, no matter how powerful the attraction between them was, a relationship could never work…could it?

He reached for his water bottle again, pouring some of the cold liquid over his head.

Damn it. Where was an ice queen when you needed one?

She must have gone temporarily mad, Livi thought as she stretched out on a daybed, enjoying the warmth of the Mediterranean sun through a fluttering canopy.

She was lying on a yacht—correction, big boat—just two months after breaking up with her long-term fiancé, with a gorgeous, currently shirtless, world-famous racing driver who she could absolutely *not* get involved with, but had already kissed. This was really not the way a professional biographer ought to behave. She was supposed to be focusing on work, on getting her life back on track, not complicating it even further, and yet here she was, wearing nothing but a bikini, a pair of large retro sunglasses—another impulse purchase—and about a gallon of suncream.

She turned her head, watching the light bounce off the water as Dario turned off the engine and came to sit beside her on the daybed. They were still in sight of land as well as a few other boats, but to all intents and purposes they were completely alone, with only the sound of the waves against the hull and a few seagulls overhead to disturb them.

Oh, yes, she'd definitely gone mad. This was blurring the lines between personal and professional a little too recklessly, and yet, despite her many, *many* misgivings, she suspected a team of wild seahorses wouldn't have been able to drag her away.

'So, what questions do you have today?' Dario asked, gesturing to the notepad lying beside her. He'd seemed more serious than usual when they'd met in the harbour that morning, though he seemed to be relaxing now they were at sea. 'I can't believe there's much more I can say about myself.'

'Actually, I have a quickfire round for you.' Livi rolled onto her stomach, reaching for her pen. 'What was your favourite race?'

'Of all my races?'

'Yes. Is there one in particular that stands out?'

'Off the top of my head…' He drew his brows

together. ‘Mexico City, four years ago. I won after starting last.’

‘Why were you starting last?’

‘A technical issue. The team had to change the power unit so I had to start the race from the pit lane.’

‘That seems harsh.’ She made a quick note. ‘So, what happened? I mean, gaining twenty places sounds fairly impressive.’

‘Thank you.’ He lay down, folding his arms behind his head. ‘But it was mainly due to the weather. The rain was so torrential, the race got red flagged twice and yellow flagged fifteen times.’

‘Hang on.’ She peered over the top of her sunglasses. ‘A red flag means the race was temporarily stopped and a yellow flag means you had to slow down and not overtake in case of hazards, right?’

‘Pretty much. So many cars went out, there were only eight of us left by the end. It evened the odds quite a lot.’

‘*That’s* your favourite race?’ She stared at him incredulously. ‘It sounds terrifying.’

‘It was a little, but I’ve always liked driving in the rain.’

‘Now I’m almost scared to ask about your worst race.’

He grimaced. ‘The whole second half of the

season two years ago was like one big, bad race. It's kind of a blur now. Looking back, I should have let the team replace me for those few months, but I didn't want to let them down. Ironically, given how badly I drove.'

She nodded sympathetically. 'Okay, moving on to something more positive. What about the future? After you hopefully win the World Championship. What next? You know, hopes, dreams, aspirations, that kind of thing.'

'Honestly, I want to keep doing what I'm doing for as long as they let me.' He twisted his face towards her. 'And when I do eventually get replaced, I'll find a way to stay in the sport somehow. Even if it's not at this level, driving is what I love.'

She nodded, fighting back a strange sad feeling, like a dull ache in her chest.

'Although maybe I can find a better work-life balance.' His expression turned introspective. 'I mean, I've never thought about it before, but if I win the championship then I guess I won't have to feel so bad about what happened two years ago any more. Maybe I won't have to be quite so career focused.'

'That makes sense.' She felt her heart skip a beat and then compensate by racing even faster.

'I guess I might even like a family some day.' He propped himself up on his elbows, looking vaguely surprised by his own words, as if he were experiencing some kind of eureka moment. 'Maybe if I was with someone who understood how much driving means to me, and that I would never intentionally neglect them, then maybe it could work. Maybe racing and relationships needn't be incompatible.' His gaze turned searching, boring into hers so intently she had the impression he was trying to see inside her head. 'How about you? What are your hopes and dreams? Do you think you'll want to try a serious relationship again some day?'

'I hope so,' she answered slowly. The air around them felt heavy all of a sudden, tense with some unspoken emotion. 'Maybe with someone who understands how I feel about my career, too.'

He hesitated, opening his mouth as if he were about to say something else, before he sat up abruptly. 'Are you hungry?'

'What?' She blinked at the change of subject.

'Are you hungry? I brought a picnic. There's Greek yogurt with fruit, some waffles and pastries, smoked salmon, asparagus wrapped in bacon…'

'Wow, yes to everything.' She pulled herself up to a sitting position. Bizarrely, the air felt normal again, as if she'd simply imagined the tension between them. 'That all sounds delicious.'

'And to drink…' He leaned past her, opening an ice box and pulling out a bottle.

'Champagne?'

'Of course. It wouldn't be a proper picnic without it.'

'That is *such* a racing driver thing to say. Hey!' She squealed as freezing water dripped from the bottle onto her legs.

'Sorry.' He chuckled, clearly not remorseful at all, already unwrapping the foil from the cork.

'Oh, you think that's funny?' She rolled over, scooping a handful of half-melted ice from the box and throwing it into his lap.

'What the—' he yelped, leaping backwards off the daybed.

'Sorry…' she mimicked him.

'Okay, that was too far.' He narrowed his eyes in mock outrage.

'What are you—' She looked at the bottle as he started to shake it up and down. 'Oh, no…'

'Oh, yes.'

'You'll soak the daybed!'

'It'll dry.'

'You wouldn't dare.'

'Wouldn't I?'

'You might hit me in the eye with the cork!'

'I won't aim it at you.'

'*Dario!*'

'*Livi.*'

'No!' She jumped to her feet, making a run for it as the bottle erupted.

'Say sorry properly!' He chased after her.

'Never!' She held her hands out in a futile attempt to defend herself, but it was no use. She was getting soaked in champagne and there was only one place to go.

Instinctively, she braced her feet and took a running jump off the front of the boat, cannonballing into the water below.

'I can't believe you just did that!' she yelled at him as she resurfaced. 'You splashed me first!'

'Mine was an accident. You upped the ante.' He grinned, his gaze following her as she swam back to the ladder.

'*And* you've wasted all our champagne!'

'I bought a spare, don't worry. Here, there's still a bit left.' He handed her the bottle as she climbed back onto the deck. 'Call it a peace offering.'

'Huh!' She stuck her tongue out, taking the bottle anyway and lifting it slowly to her mouth.

'How was the water?' he asked, his eyes following the movement. There was something searing about his gaze now, she noticed, something that made her breath quicken all over again. Even in the sunlight, his pupils seemed swollen to black orbs.

'Cooling.' She licked her lips. 'I thought you said you didn't like bubbles?'

'I don't.' His voice sounded deeper than usual. 'Although I might be changing my mind.'

She swallowed. The air was thick again, meaningful in a way that was definitely *not* work-related, only right now she had a score to settle… Slowly, she passed the bottle back, waiting until he set it aside before grasping the railing with one hand and his wrist with the other, using her body weight to heave him headlong into the sea behind her.

'Now we're even!' she shouted, laughing as he shook his head like a dog.

'Ha!' He splashed water at her. 'I suppose I deserved that.'

'Yes, you did.' She smiled coyly, crouching down beside the ladder as he swam towards it. 'Do you want a towel?'

'No.' He heaved himself upwards, forearms flexing and chest streaming with water as he brought his face level with hers.

'Oh…' She felt her mouth turn dry. 'I guess it's picnic time, then?'

'Livi.' He caught at her arm, pulling her back as she started to move away.

She froze, feeling a shiver of anticipation at

the intensity of his expression. It was intoxicating, making her feel tingly and light-headed. It was clearly affecting her limbs too, since she seemed unable to move or do anything except stare back at him.

She couldn't remember the last time a man had looked at her with such naked desire. If she was completely honest, she didn't think Matthew ever had. She felt as though Dario's gaze was sinking into her skin, piercing all the way through to her heart. And then she was leaning forward and he was lifting his hands, skimming the backs of his fingers lightly across her cheeks and bringing his mouth down to hers.

Her eyelids fluttered closed. She tasted champagne and salt and something citrusy all wrapped into one heady combination, simultaneously delicious and invigorating.

'Is this all right?' he murmured against her mouth. 'Or does it make you want to jump back in the sea?'

She tilted her head in reply, adjusting the angle of the kiss while she raised her hands to his chest, spreading her fingers out over his pectoral muscles. His skin felt warm to the touch, silky smooth and yet hard too. No, she didn't want to jump anywhere, except maybe into his arms.

There were still so many reasons why this

was a bad idea, but at that moment she seemed unable to articulate any of them. Her body was boneless and weightless, as if she was floating in the water again. The world beyond the boat ceased to exist as his fingers tangled in her hair and she touched her tongue to the seam of his mouth, nudging his lips apart so she could explore inside. They kept on kissing, neither of them wanting to break apart, even as he climbed over the top of the ladder, pulling her to her feet and towards the daybed.

They landed heavily, wet limbs tangling and writhing together as they rolled over and over, stroking and caressing and exploring each other's body. She arched her back, making a whimpering sound as he slid the straps of her bikini down her arms, nuzzling the newly exposed skin underneath, before trailing a path of kisses between her breasts and over her stomach, sending thrills of sensation skittering up and down her spine.

'Livi…' he murmured, his voice a light rumble against her stomach, and she gave a low moan in response, heat erupting between her legs. 'You're so beautiful.'

'So are you.' She sucked in a breath. This might be crazy, but it felt right, natural, inevitable almost, as if she'd been waiting her whole life for just this moment. She could feel an ache building inside her, not just physical but emotional, too, as if nothing mattered but this. Them.

Them?

A surge of panic swept through her. What was she doing? There was no *them*. There couldn't be. She'd sworn off men and relationships only two months ago! How could she risk getting hurt all over again when she'd barely recovered from Matthew's betrayal? And with a man she knew was also capable of deceit. Especially when the way she felt about Dario was beginning to feel like more than simply attraction and more like…love?

Love? Her mind baulked at the idea. How could she have developed such powerful feelings for him, so quickly? Yes, he was a hundred times better than the media gave him credit for, but he hadn't mentioned anything about feelings for *her*. There had been nothing to suggest he wanted to see her again in the future, or that he thought of her as a potential partner, except maybe the way he'd looked at her when he'd talked about having a better work-life balance one day, but she could easily have read too much into that, and the words themselves could have been purely theoretical. What if, for him, this was nothing more than lust and opportunity, involving no deeper emotions at all? What if she was in real danger of falling head over heels for a man who would only forget her in a week's time?

She stiffened, her mind spinning with *what ifs* and *maybes*, because even if she was being unfair and this meant something to him too, how could she go through with it? She'd be jeopardising her career, the one good thing that Matthew had left her. Never mind Dario's career. What if he'd been right the first time about racing and relationships being incompatible and this—*them*—somehow destroyed his chance at the championship? She'd never forgive herself. Their whole situation was too complicated and way, *way* out of control. All of which meant they had to stop, no matter how much she yearned to keep going…

'Livi?' Dario lifted his head. 'What's wrong?'

'I can't do this.' She closed her eyes, afraid to look at him in case she changed her mind again. 'This—*us*—it can't work. We agreed. We both have too much to lose.'

'You're right.' His breath was still coming fast. 'I'm sorry. I didn't mean to…'

'I know.'

'I just wish…' He stayed completely still for a few seconds, before she felt him pull away. 'It won't happen again, I promise.'

She twisted her face aside, struck with the horrible feeling that she was losing her heart anyway.

Dario gripped the steering wheel, feeling something twist in his chest as they sailed back into the harbour. A swift glance over his shoulder showed Livi sitting on one side of the boat, a white knitted dress covering her bikini now, bare feet curled up beneath her as she gazed out to sea, a faintly wistful expression on her face.

After an almost painfully polite picnic, they'd been mostly silent on the journey back, the tension between them still palpable. He couldn't stop remembering the way she'd felt and tasted, gasping and writhing beneath him, as though those few minutes were etched into his brain. His whole body ached to hold her again, but she'd been right. It couldn't happen, not now, when he had the World Championship almost within touching distance. He couldn't let himself lose focus, even if he had a sneaking suspicion it was already too late for that.

'Dario.' She came to stand beside him as he moored the boat. 'Thank you. For the picnic and…everything.'

'You're welcome.' He forced a smile to his lips. 'I guess I'll see you at my apartment tomorrow morning?'

'Actually…' her expression wavered and then turned resolute '…I don't think we need to meet again. You've answered all of my questions.'

'Already?' His stomach felt as if there was a block of ice inside it. 'But we have two more days.'

'I know, but I have everything I need.' She sounded formal, the way she had in their very first interview. She'd even tied her hair back again, he noticed. 'If anything else comes up, I'll reach out through Ethan.'

'Livi—' he frowned '—what happened today doesn't have to ruin things.'

'I know, but if I stay it might happen again, and I think…' her voice wavered '…I think this is the best thing for both of us.'

He clenched his jaw, fighting the urge to wrap his arms around her and stop her from leaving. 'I understand. But you don't have to contact Ethan if you need anything. You can just call me.'

She nodded jerkily. 'In that case, I guess this is goodbye?'

'I guess so.' He thought about holding a hand out and then decided against it. Just standing this close to her was painful. Touching her and then having to let go again would be unbearable.

'There was just one more thing I wanted to say.' She rearranged her satchel on her arm, as if she was trying to be businesslike again. 'Kind of a suggestion, if you don't mind?'

'Go on.'

'It's about Karolina. I think you should invite her to your next race. Jean-Michel, too, if possible. If people see you together as friends, it might make them realise how judgemental they've been about your relationship.'

'She needs to focus on her baby.'

'Isn't that her decision?' She jutted her chin up. 'I think she wants to do it. She wants to help. And the next race is in Italy, isn't it? So she wouldn't have to travel far. Maybe just think about it?'

'Okay,' he relented. 'I'll talk to her about it. For you.'

'Thank you.' She paused and then reached into her bag, pulling out the pebble she'd shown him on the evening of their first kiss in his apartment and placing it next to the steering wheel. 'I know it's not much of a goodbye gift, but I want you to have this. My sister said I should give it back once the book was finished, but this way you'll know you're not just a stepping stone to me, not any more.' She gave a tight smile. 'Goodbye, Dario. I really hope you win the championship.'

'Wait,' he called out when she was two steps away. 'Will I see you again?'

'I don't know.' She stopped briefly, half turning her head, though she didn't look back. 'Camille will be in touch about the book.'

CHAPTER SIXTEEN

Three months later

'WELCOME HOME!' Chloe flung open the door to Livi's flat with a huge smile. 'You know, this is becoming a habit. First Monaco, now Paris. How was it?'

'Wonderful. I ate my own body weight in patisserie.' Livi gave her a reunion hug before heaving her small suitcase inside. 'Wow, you've tidied up. This place looks great.'

'You were only gone for five days.' Her sister put her hands on her hips defensively. 'Plus, I cleaned up this morning. Thanks for letting me stay again, by the way. I really appreciate it.'

'No problem. You know, you can always escape here.'

'You might regret saying that.' Chloe winked. 'Now, come on through, I put the kettle on the moment you texted from the tube station.'

'Perfect. Parisian coffee is gorgeous, but

their tea just isn't the same.' Livi pulled off her black belted trench coat before quickly checking her reflection. After four months of sunflower blonde, she'd recently switched to mocha mousse, a shade closer to her own natural hair colour, though she still got a small shock every time she glanced in a mirror.

'So, how are you feeling now that you're officially unemployed?' Chloe asked, nudging a steaming mug and plate of biscuits towards her as they sat down at the small kitchen table. 'Try an orange and cardamom cookie. I baked them this morning. There's no sugar, just honey, so they're practically a health food.'

'Thanks.' Livi reached for the biggest. 'But, for the record, I'm not unemployed yet. I got an email from Dario's team approving all of my revisions, but I won't know if the book's officially signed off until I see Camille tomorrow.'

'But it's still being released next month, right? Isn't that cutting it a little fine?'

'Definitely, but they're fast-tracking everything.'

Chloe's eyes sparkled. 'Does that mean you'll be invited to some big, glamorous launch event?'

'Probably.' Her heart stuttered at the thought. 'But even if I am, I'm not sure I'll go. I'm not exactly the one people want to see.'

'That's so unfair. You're the writer.'

'It's how it is.' She took a sip of tea to hide her expression. She'd told Chloe that Dario had been much nicer than the media gave him credit for, whilst omitting several key details about their time together, possibly because she suspected her sister would tell her she'd been insane to walk away, which was quite possibly true. It was the very question she'd gone to Paris to ask herself, impulsively booking a seat on the Eurostar once she'd finally hit Send on her revised manuscript. The City of Love had seemed like the perfect, albeit slightly masochistic, place to think about him.

'Well, at least him being World Champion now should guarantee good sales,' Chloe went on. 'That must be a relief, right?'

'Mmm-hmm.' Livi put her mug down again. Dario had won the first race after the summer break in Italy, where he'd posted a photo of Karolina and Jean-Michel celebrating with him on his social media, before he'd officially clinched the championship a month later, in Brazil. As pleased as she'd been about that, she'd been just as pleased with the photo. It had felt like a private message to her, a sign that he valued her advice. She'd been tempted to contact him again on both occasions, but managed to restrain herself, knowing it would only cause her more heartache. To her surprise and delight, however, Karolina had messaged her separately in October, sharing pictures of her new baby, a beautiful girl called Miranda Sylvie.

'How are you feeling now?' Chloe asked, tipping her head to one side with a faintly worried expression. 'I mean, you've had a rough few months, thanks to Matthew.'

'Matthew's in the past,' Livi answered honestly, since her mind had been far more preoccupied with a different man recently. 'I spent a lot of time in Paris just walking and thinking and now I genuinely believe he did me a favour, in a messed-up kind of way. We'd grown apart, but I didn't want to admit it. I feel better about myself now than I have in a long time.'

'Well, that's great.' Chloe clinked their tea mugs together. 'I'm really happy for you, sis.'

'I'm happy for me too.' Livi smiled, despite the now familiar ache in her chest. As happy as she was *for* herself, feeling it inside was a different matter. After spending so much time immersed in writing, Paris had finally given her a chance to decompress and process her emotions, and now, as much as she knew she'd done the right thing by protecting her heart and her career, as well as Dario's, she couldn't help but also regret what she'd potentially given up in Monaco.

After having some time to think of him as *Dario*, the man she'd come to know, not just the subject of her book, she realised she'd been unfair, comparing his deceit to Matthew's. He might have misled her about Karolina, but he'd done it for all the right reasons. In fact, he'd shown her time and again that he was nothing like the way he was portrayed in the media. There was nothing villainous about him. He was kind and loyal and thoughtful and trustworthy, and as hard as she'd tried to fall out of love with him over the past three months, she knew she still hadn't succeeded. Maybe if they'd met at some other point in their lives, things could have been different, but she'd made her choice and now she had to live with it. The most frustrating part was that she still had no idea how he felt about her, and even if their paths did cross again at some publishing event, it wasn't the kind of question you could just blurt out…

'What about you?' she asked, pulling her mind back to the present. 'Has anything exciting happened here over the last week?'

'Just one thing. I quit my job.'

'What?' Livi gave a jolt, almost spilling her tea.

'I'm setting up as a personal trainer and physiotherapist all on my own.' Chloe sounded excited. 'I've been building my online profile for a while, and I decided it was time to stop thinking and start doing.' She gestured to the plate on the table. 'These cookies are actually gifts for new clients. Part of a wellness package I'm devising to help people switch to healthier homemade snacks.'

'That's a brilliant idea.' Livi beamed. 'Chloe, I'm so pleased for you.'

'So, I wondered if your offer still stands? About me moving in? I know you said it's only a sofa bed, but that might be all I can afford for a while. Plus, I've got so much more done this week without all the noise and mess where I live. I've decided to take myself seriously and act like a grown-up from now on, you know with early nights and clean kitchens and all that stuff.'

'Wow, you make me sound so fun.' Livi laughed. 'Of course you can move in.'

'Thank you, and you *are* fun. You just took yourself off to Paris for a week on the spur of the moment.' Chloe reached for another biscuit. 'By the way, if you're seeing your agent tomorrow, does that mean you'll find out about the Erin Cole book, as well?'

'Hopefully.' Livi crossed her fingers.

'That's so exciting. Can I take you out for dinner tonight to pre-emptively celebrate?'

'No, *I'm* taking *you* out to celebrate your

news!' Livi reached across the table to give her another hug. 'Just let me grab a quick shower and I'll be all yours.'

'Livi, you look well,' Camille commented, looking her up and down with an approving expression as she greeted her the next morning. 'Usually when you've just finished a book, you look like you need to sleep for a month, but it's like you've just come from a spa.'

'Paris, actually.' Livi held out a box. 'These are for you. Macaroons.'

'My favourites, thank you.' Camille gestured towards a chair. 'What took you to Paris?'

'I just wanted a holiday. You know, a change of scene to clear my head and recharge.'

'Good idea. The last few months must have been pretty intense.'

'You could say that. So...' Livi perched nervously on the edge of her seat '...do you have good news?'

'About the book? Better than good. Personally, I think it's your best. Insightful, balanced and surprisingly compelling for a non-sports fan like myself. Considering how reluctant you were to take on the project, you've done an amazing job.' She smiled warmly. 'I have to say, I was particularly impressed with the way you handled his personal life. You did what he asked and kept his marriage and divorce mostly out of it, whilst subtly undermining a few of those old rumours too. His management team are delighted.'

'Great.' She heaved a sigh of relief. It was ironic that the project she'd cared about the least to begin with had become the one that meant the most, but, after three months of hard work, she'd been pleased with the way it had turned out, and with her professional integrity mostly intact. Yes, she'd been a little biased—okay, a lot—but she could honestly say that she'd been as objective as possible under the circumstances.

'So, is that it? Am I officially done with the project?'

'You are. Congratulations.' Camille's smile wavered. 'Although I'm afraid I have some bad news, too. Apparently, Erin Cole's had second thoughts about writing a biography. It seems like that project won't be going ahead, after all.'

'Oh.' Livi sat back in her chair, needing a moment to process her emotions. The chance of working with Erin had been the main reason she'd taken on Dario's book, and yet now that it wasn't going to happen she felt…surprisingly okay. Disappointed, yes, but not devastated. Writing Erin's biography would have been the pinnacle of her career, yes, but not her life, because her life was more than her career.

She experienced a moment of sudden, sharp clarity. Matthew might have made her feel like her work was all she had left, but Matthew was long gone and, somewhere along the way, she'd got her self-esteem and confidence back. Largely thanks to Dario. His book hadn't led her to Erin. It had led her back to herself, and that was much, much better. As for all the life advice she'd hoped to get from Erin…well, she was still interested, but she didn't *need* it any more.

'I'm really sorry, Livi.' Camille sounded anxious.

'Don't be.' She shook her head. 'The Erin book was never a certainty. There'll be other projects.'

'Wow.' Her agent's eyebrows shot up. 'I was afraid you might take my macaroons back.'

'It's not your fault. People are allowed to change their minds.'

'Well, Dario's book is going to do wonders for your profile anyway. Erin aside, you'll be able to have your pick of future projects.'

'Great. Let me know if anything exciting comes up, but don't expect a quick reply. I think I need a bit more of a break before I commit to my next project.'

'I completely understand. You must feel burnt out, but at least now you can sit back and let the publisher take over. There's a lot happening already. From what I've heard, Dario's meeting them today for some publicity shots.'

'Today?' She stiffened as though she'd just had an electric shock. 'You mean Dario's in London?'

'Apparently. We're actually invited to join them, if you'd like?' Camille glanced at her watch. 'I have a couple of hours free.'

'Right now?' Her stomach felt as if it was flipping over and tying itself in knots simultaneously.

Did she want to see him? Yes! She was already halfway out of her chair at the thought. Now that she'd realised her work wasn't everything it occurred to her that she didn't need to care about her professional reputation so much any more, and it wasn't as though she could ruin Dario's World Championship chances when he'd already won. Maybe there was a chance for them, after all. Maybe they could be together and let all of the other stuff work itself out.

On the other hand, she realised, coming back down to earth with a bump, there was still Dario's reputation to consider. The last thing she wanted was to give the media anything else to attack him with. And what if he hadn't missed her in the way she'd missed him? What if he hadn't missed her at all? What if he'd practically forgotten her? In which case, wasn't it better to leave things as they were? Then, as much as she might always wonder about what might have been, at least she wouldn't ruin the memory of their time together. She had her equilibrium and confidence back. Why risk losing all of that again?

'Livi?' Camille's head was cocked to one side.

'Sorry.' She blinked, realising that she'd been staring into thin air for a few seconds. 'Do you know who invited us? Was it Dario himself or the publisher?'

'I don't know.' Camille looked confused. 'I mean, the message was from the publisher, but I suppose it could have come from him.'

She sucked her bottom lip into her mouth, trying to decide what to do. If the message had come from Dario then surely that meant he wanted to see her again, but if it was just from the publisher...well, that could be awkward. Potentially even heart-breaking. And it would be hard enough to act normally with people and cameras around them.

'Actually, I don't think I'm in the mood, but please thank them anyway.'

'No problem. You must be sick to your back teeth of thinking about Dario Xydis.'

'Right.' She tried to sound nonchalant as she reached for her bag, suddenly eager to be going. 'Is that everything?'

'I suppose so.' Camille looked taken aback. 'Just let me know when you're ready to get back to work and we'll go for lunch.'

'I will. Thanks!'

She practically ran out of the office and towards the lifts, her mind whirling. She needed to know if the message had come from Dario, but she definitely didn't want to find out the answer in public. No, she needed to ask somebody else—somebody who might know how he felt about her.

Fortunately, she knew just who to call.

CHAPTER SEVENTEEN

DARIO PULLED UP outside a Mayfair hotel, handing the keys of his Lotus Evija to a valet as he climbed out. The publicity photoshoot had taken three hours, four outfit changes and a near falling-out with the director, who'd kept asking him to smile and relax like a man who'd recently won the World Championship, not one who kept glancing at the door as if he was expecting someone. Apparently, the original concept had undergone some emergency revisions.

He unbuttoned his suit jacket as he strode into the hotel alongside Ethan. It hadn't been the director's fault, of course. It was London's. Being here, so close to Livi, was maddening. It seemed ironic that he'd been so obsessed with *not* getting distracted by her when he'd been nothing but for the past three months. Even more ironically, it hadn't affected his driving either; he supposed all the counselling after his divorce had finally sunk in. That had been a huge relief, obviously, but he'd missed Livi so much that even winning the World Championship had felt almost like second best.

He hadn't appreciated the full strength of his feelings for her, and what a mistake he'd made, until she'd left Monaco. It had taken him a while to process, to realise that just because he'd failed in relationships in the past didn't mean he'd inevitably fail again, especially with someone whose career mattered to her as much as his did to him. Maybe that made them compatible. Hell, maybe it even made them perfect for each other.

Now it was taking all his willpower not to call her agent, find out where she lived and go to find her. The only thing stopping him was the ferocious schedule Ethan had him following. That and her non-appearance today. He'd sent the invitation via his publisher in the hope she might seize the opportunity to stop by, but there hadn't been so much as a text. As hints went, it was a pretty strong one. Clearly, she hadn't changed her mind about them, and he had to respect that.

'How long do we have before this dinner with the publishers tonight?' he asked Ethan as they walked through the granite stone lobby.

'Actually, I'm not sure that's still going

ahead.' Ethan's tone was uncharacteristically vague. 'It might be cancelled.'

'Really?' He pursed his brows. 'People were talking about it at the photoshoot. It sounded like it was still on.'

'Well, nothing's decided yet. There's somebody who needs to speak with you in the lounge first.'

'Who?'

'You'll know who I mean.' Ethan lifted his phone to his ear, waving a hand as he veered off in the opposite direction. 'I'll just be a minute.'

Dario heaved a sigh as he headed for the lounge. He wasn't in the mood for another meeting, and what did *'You'll know who I mean'* mean? Ethan wasn't usually so evasive.

He stopped in the doorway and looked around, his gaze skimming impatiently past the pianist in one corner, then over the scattering of sofas and tables. It was reasonably busy for early evening, but he didn't see anyone he recognised.

Great. He rolled his eyes and made for the bar, slipping onto a leather stool next to a woman in black with warm brown hair falling in glossy waves to her shoulders. Whoever Ethan meant, they could come and find him. In the meantime, he was going to order a drink and—

'Hi.'

He froze at the sound of Livi's voice, half afraid to look round in case he was imagining things.

'Dario?' She sounded hesitant.

He turned finally, sucking in a breath at the sight of her. 'Livi. You're…' He wasn't sure what to say. 'I didn't recognise you.'

She touched a hand to her hair. 'I decided I wanted to look like myself again.'

'It looks good.' He cleared his throat. 'You look good.'

'Thank you.'

'Why didn't you come to the photoshoot?' The question came out sounding more confrontational than he'd intended, but now she was there, right beside him, he wasn't sure how to behave and he didn't want to get his hopes up. For all he knew, this was yet another work meeting.

'Honestly?' Her voice wobbled slightly. 'I didn't know if the invitation came from you or the publisher, and then I thought, either way, it would probably be better for us to talk in private.'

'About the book?'

'No-o. My work on that is finished. I've fulfilled my side of the contract, so our working relationship is officially over.'

'So, this is a personal meeting?' He twisted his stool round towards her.

'Yes.' She paused. 'Although I'd understand if you'd rather keep it professional.'

'I don't.' He slid a hand across the bar, until his fingers were just touching hers. 'I've thought about you every day since you walked off my boat.'

'You have?' Green eyes flickered. 'I've thought about you too, and not just because I had to for work. I've thought about you the rest of the time too. It's been…'

'Driving you crazy?' He slid his thumb over the back of her hand, gently caressing the knuckles.

'Yes.' She drew her tongue between her lips, as if she needed to moisten them. 'Congratulations on being a world champion, by the way.'

'Thank you.' He lifted an eyebrow. 'What about you? Did you get that other project you wanted? The Erin Cole book?'

'Actually, no. She's decided against a biography.'

'I'm sorry. I know how much it meant to you.'

'It did, and I guess it still does in a way, but a lot of things have changed since the summer.' She swallowed, a series of emotions flickering over her face. 'Look, there's something I want to say, and it might be too much, but I just need to say it, okay?'

'Okay.'

'The thing is…' She took a deep breath. 'When Matthew and I broke up, I felt completely rejected. I'd put so much into our relationship, it was like all I had left was my career. Then I met you and I started to feel better about myself. I got my confidence back, but then… I guess I was afraid of getting hurt and losing it again, plus my career too. It all happened so fast, and I was scared to trust you, but if it's not too late…'

'It's not.' He lifted his hand to her cheek. 'I was scared to trust you, too. I was so afraid of the past repeating itself, I thought I had to be alone to win, but then, when I did win, all I could think about was how much I wished you were there to share it with me. I guess we both had issues to work out.'

She leaned her face into his hand, her lips parting, just as a barman appeared beside them.

'Can I get you anything, sir?'

'Not right now.' He didn't take his gaze away from hers, waiting until the barman had moved away before speaking again. 'What about the book? You were right—if people find out about us before it's published, it could damage your reputation.'

'And yours, but if you're prepared to take the risk, so am I.' She threw a quick glance around the room. 'You know, there are quite a few people trying to pretend they're not watching us right now. I think you've been recognised.'

'They'll probably start filming in a moment.' He lifted his eyes skyward and then leaned closer, bringing his lips close to her ear. 'How much of a stir do you think it would cause if I kissed you?'

'I don't care.' Her eyes flickered past him. 'Although your manager might not approve.'

'Sorry to interrupt.' Ethan came to stand between them. 'So, I guess I'm cancelling dinner?'

Dario nodded. 'Tell them I'm going to be busy tomorrow as well.'

'You know, as your manager I should really object, but as your friend…' Ethan grinned. 'I guess I'll see you in a couple of days?'

'At least.'

'But you owe me for all the trouble this is going to cause.'

'Anything you want.'

'Good.' Ethan put a hand on each of their shoulders. 'In that case, you can start by taking this reunion somewhere a little more private. You look like you're about to jump on each other.'

'He makes a good point.' Livi climbed off

her stool, holding a hand out to Dario, as Ethan coughed and turned away. 'How about we go to your room instead?'

'We don't have to,' he forced himself to murmur, his skin already prickling at the idea of being alone with her. 'I can wait.'

'But I can't.' She slid her fingers between his, lacing them together as she pulled him after her. 'I think it's time we proved how much we've missed each other.'

Livi slipped her arms around Dario's neck, drawing his mouth down to hers the moment the door closed behind them, a moan catching in her throat as his familiar scent enveloped her. Now they were finally alone, her need for him was almost unbearable, as though she'd been starving herself for the past three months.

She'd gone home to shower and change after she'd called Ethan, putting on her laciest underwear beneath a little black dress. She hadn't known how Dario would react to seeing her again, but she'd wanted to be prepared just in case, and now, hearing his sharp intake of breath as his hands slid beneath her hem, she was extremely glad that she had.

'I feel like we should take this slowly.' His voice sounded strained as he nuzzled his face into her neck, pressing open-mouthed kisses all the way from behind her ear down to her collarbone. 'But I'm not sure I can.'

'We can go slow next time.' She caught the lobe of his ear between her teeth before pushing herself away from the door, already reaching behind to unfasten the clasp of her dress. 'We've waited long enough.'

They unzipped and unbuttoned their way across the room, leaving puddles of garments behind them until they reached the bed, an almost frantic quality to their movements as Livi fell on top of the mattress and he crawled between her legs, caging her there.

She lay back, vividly aware of every small detail of the room around them, the silky touch of the sheets, the low hum of the air-conditioning, the ragged sound of their breathing and the moist touch of his mouth. She'd imagined this scene often enough, but it was still more intense than anything she'd anticipated, as if all her senses were being pushed to breaking point. Pulses of sensation were rippling up and down her spine, turning her insides to liquid. She dug her fingers into the bedsheets, her body humming, utterly consumed by desire, as if the rest of the world no longer existed and they were the only two people left, alone in this bed.

'You have no…idea how much… I missed you.' The words vibrated through her body as he licked his way hungrily over her skin, causing a coiling, tightening sensation low down in her abdomen.

'I missed…you too…' she gasped, her breath coming in hot raspy bursts as he moved lower, wanting to draw the moment out and rush onwards at the same time. She felt coiled so tight, she thought she might burst otherwise. 'Do you have protection?'

He stopped abruptly, muttering something she didn't understand before lifting his head, dark eyes burning with a horrified expression.

'It's okay.' She almost laughed. 'I brought some, just in case.'

'Now you tell me.' He exhaled loudly. 'I think my heart just stopped beating.'

'Don't go anywhere.' She wriggled off the bed, scampering back to the door to find her purse.

Less than a minute later, she was back, straddling him as he slid the condom over his erection.

'Wait.' He caught at her waist, fingers twitching as if he were restraining himself with an effort. 'Are you certain?'

She answered by lowering her body onto his, moaning as he filled her.

'Livi…'

Air hissed between his teeth as his hands

tightened around her hips, holding her at just the right angle as she rocked back and forth, arching her back and rolling against him until…

Oh, no... She bit her lip, trying to control the rhythm and restrain her body's response as her inner muscles clenched. It was too soon, too fast, but she was already too far gone to hold back, powerless to do anything but throw her head back and cry out as her vision blurred and her body pulsed around him. Her climax came even harder than she'd expected, pushing any attempt at coherent thought out of her head as wave upon wave of sensation washed over and through her.

'Livi?' He pushed himself upwards, curling one arm around her waist as she sagged against him.

'Don't stop.' She smiled, shivers of feeling still racing over her skin as he flipped them over and pushed even deeper inside her, then gathered her in his arms as he thrust one last time and shuddered.

'Livi—' he panted her name, his forehead pressed against her shoulder '—I missed you *that* much.'

'No regrets?' Dario wheeled the room service trolley to the edge of the bed.

'None.' She gave him a teasing look. 'Why?

Are you over me now? Was this just a physical thing, after all?'

'It's *definitely* a physical thing.' He chuckled as he slid back under the covers, hauling her into his arms. 'But it's a lot more than that, too. As for getting over you…' He waggled his eyebrows. 'That might take a while. A lifetime possibly.'

'That's a pretty good start.' She snuggled into his arms and gave a long, lingering sigh of contentment. 'What did you order?'

'Just a few high energy foods. I hope you weren't planning on getting much sleep tonight.'

'Not a wink.'

'Perfect.' He pressed a kiss to the top of her head. 'I wish we could just stay here until after the book comes out. Then we wouldn't have to worry about how anyone will react to us being a couple.'

'You mean, stay in bed for the next month?'

'Sounds good to me. I have a lot of stamina.'

'Well, it *is* a nice bed, and I love the idea of your stamina, but that might not be entirely practical.' She rolled onto her stomach, so that she was lying between his legs, her breasts pressed against his chest. 'Don't you still have two races left?'

'Damn. I knew I was forgetting something.'

'Not to mention publicity to do. It's my book as well, after all. I want it to be a success.'

'Another good point.' He trailed a path down her spine with his fingertips.

'Besides, I don't care what anyone thinks about us any more. We know the truth, that's all that matters.'

'In that case, there's only one thing for it. You'll need to do all the publicity with me. We've spent enough time apart.'

'If that's what you want…' She smiled, her cheeks suffusing with heat as his hands curved around her bottom, pressing her even closer against him. 'Fortunately, my schedule is wide open. I could even come to your races since I can't mess up your championship chances any more.'

'You still almost did.'

'Excuse me?' She blinked. 'What's that supposed to mean?'

'Ethan says I've been distracted for the past three months. "Like a lovesick puppy" were his exact words.'

'Lovesick?' She sucked in a breath, feeling as though there wasn't enough air in the room suddenly.

'Yes. Unless that's too big a word?'

'No. I think it's the perfect word.' She smiled.

'You know, I was afraid you might have forgotten me.'

'As if I could.' He looked deep into her eyes. 'I never expected to feel this way about anybody again.'

'Nor did I.'

'You know I'm saying I love you, right?'

'I do.' She leaned forward, tipping her forehead against his. 'I'm a writer. I can read between the lines. And I love you, too.'

'So, this is it, we're official?'

'Yes, we are. Although, I have to say, I'm a little disappointed.'

His face clouded instantly. 'Why?'

'Because you're a racing driver and you still haven't driven me anywhere. We haven't even been in a car together.'

'You're right.' He looked faintly stunned. 'Okay, we need to fix that. As soon as the season is finished, we're going on a road trip.' His lips curved again. 'Incidentally, have you ever been to Australia?'

EPILOGUE

Two months later

'OKAY, I'M READY!' Livi called out, sliding on a pair of diamond drop earrings as she emerged from the bedroom of Dario's Sydney apartment, wearing a black and white ruffle-sleeved mini-dress, her hair in a half up, half down braided bun. 'All dressed up, as instructed.'

'Wow.' Dario glanced up from where he was lying, sprawled on the couch. 'You look amazing.'

'Thank you.' She made a mock curtsey. '*Now* will you tell me why we're still in Sydney? I thought we were going to stay with your parents for a few days before we drive the coast road to Adelaide?'

'We'll go to my parents' tomorrow. This is just a temporary delay. One day only, I promise.'

'*Because?*'

'Because you have a lunch date.'

'*I* have a lunch date? What about you?' She narrowed her eyes suspiciously. 'You know you're being weirdly secretive.'

'So many questions.' He shook his head as he walked slowly towards her. 'Anyone would think you were writing a sequel to my life story.'

'You know very well, I'm on a work hiatus.' She put her hands on her hips as he buried his face in her neck. 'And don't think you can distract me that easily.'

'Pity.' He chuckled and reached for one of her hands, tugging her towards the door. 'Come on, then. The sooner we go, the sooner all of this will make sense.'

'Am I allowed to know how far we have to walk, at least?' she asked as they stepped out into the dazzling late-morning sunshine. It was summer in the southern hemisphere and the temperature was pushing twenty-five degrees, although thankfully a sea breeze made the air bearable.

'Not far, I promise.'

'Good. Because I'm still tired from all our sightseeing yesterday.' She nudged him with her elbow. 'It didn't help that *somebody* didn't let me sleep much last night.'

'As I recall, somebody *else* woke me up this morning.' He lifted her hand to his lips, pressing a kiss to her knuckles. 'Not that I'm complaining. You can wake me up like that any time you want.'

'That might depend on whether I like this surprise or not.'

'Oh, you will.' He shot her a smug grin. 'Trust me.'

They walked hand in hand across Pyrmont Bridge and into the Darling Harbour district, past the aquarium towards the King Street Wharf. Despite being a new national hero, Dario somehow managed to stay anonymous in a baseball cap and large sunglasses, blending in with the crowd so well that only a couple of people gave double takes as they walked past.

'Here we are.' He stopped finally, outside a glass-fronted restaurant on the waterfront.

'This looks nice.' Livi looked speculatively at the building. It was low and futuristic-looking, with a collection of pots filled with ornamental grasses around the terrace, giving the space an elegant, relaxed atmosphere. 'Are you coming inside to introduce me?'

'No need. You already know the person pretty well.' He tilted his head. 'Sort of.'

'Sort of?'

'Okay, look.' He looped his hands around her waist. 'I don't want to interfere. I mean, obviously, I am interfering a little, but I also want you to know, there's no obligation here, not for either of you. I just set this thing up. The rest is completely up to you.'

'You're making no sense.' She lifted her hands to his chest. 'Dario, what are you talking about?'

'Remember how you told me that writing Erin Cole's biography was your dream project?'

'Yes.'

'Well, she came to a race last season as a guest of the team.'

'You met her?' Livi gaped at him. 'Wait, was this before or after the summer break?'

'After. It was a total coincidence, I promise, but she was friendly, so when I heard that her tour was coming to Australia at the same time we were going to be here, I got in contact. I said I'd heard that she was considering a biography, and I knew the perfect person to write it.'

'But I thought she'd decided against it?'

'She had, but I think she's wavering, so I told her that you were a consummate professional and how much you love her work.'

'That's… I mean, I don't know what to say.' She caught her breath. 'Hang on, does she know about us?'

'Of course. We're a power couple now, remember?'

'Urgh.' She rolled her eyes. 'You know I still have mixed feelings about that. I can't believe the press made such a big thing of us being together.'

'At least it wasn't in the way we expected. We couldn't have planned a better PR campaign. My reputation has been restored through love and yours has gone stratospheric. I'm not a villain any more and you're a bestseller.'

'*We're* a bestseller.' She worried at her bottom lip. 'But right now, I'm just nervous.'

'Don't be. You'll be great. Just try and enjoy the lunch. It's on me so order as much champagne as you want.' He smiled reassuringly. 'Even if nothing comes of this, at least you still get to meet her.'

'That's true.'

'Now, go and show her how amazing you are.'

'Wait! Are you sure about this?' She caught at one of his hands as he started to move away. 'I mean, what if she does hire me? The racing season starts again soon. What if we both get so focused on our work that we end up growing apart?'

'We'll definitely both get focused on our work, but we won't grow apart. We'll make sure of it.' He bent to kiss her nose. 'Us workaholics need to stick together.'

'Okay.' She sucked in a deep breath, drawing her shoulders back. 'How do I look?'

'Like a sexy librarian ice queen.'

'I was going for relaxed.'

'Too bad.' He grinned. 'You'll always be a sexy librarian ice queen to me.'

* * * * *

If you enjoyed this story, check out these other great reads from Jenni Fletcher

A Marquess to Remember
A Wedding to Protect Her Fortune
Cinderella's Deal with the Colonel
The Shopgirl's Forbidden Love

All available now!